From the Mountains to the River:

Mostly True Stories Worth the Tellin'

Suellen Alfred

And

Joyce Milligan Tatum

Mossy Creek PRESS

Mossy Creek Press

From the Mountains to the River: Mostly True Stories Worth the Tellin'

ISBN: Softcover 978-0-692-53702-2

Copyright © 2015 by Suellen Alfred and Joyce Milligan Tatum

To order additional copies of this book, contact:

Mossy Creek Press

1-423-475-7308

www.mossycreekpress.com

Mossy Creek Press is an imprint of Parson's Porch & Company (PP&C) in Cleveland, Tennessee. PP&C is an innovative non-profit organization which raises money by publishing books of noted authors, representing all genres. All donations from contributors and profits from publishing are shared with the poor.

From the Mountains to the River:

Mostly True Stories Worth the Tellin'

This book is dedicated to the memory of our parents

Freeda and Andrew Alfred

and to

Jeff and Mattie Milligan

Our very first storytellers

and to

Alan Tatum

a very supportive husband

Acknowledgements

We are grateful to the men and women who have allowed us to include their personal stories in this book.

Thanks to Betty Roe and Sandy Smith for permission to use a few stories from the book, *Teaching Through Stories: Yours, Mine, and Theirs*. Norwood, Massachusetts: Christopher-Gordon, 1998.

Most of all we thank our families and friends who have patiently listened to us talk about this book as it was taking shape. Now, at long last, they will have a chance to read it.

Table of Contents

Introduction

When we started swapping stories with each other, we realized our stories are poignant enough, interesting enough, and funny enough to share with others. That is how this book got started and ultimately came to fruition. Oddly, we are really very different in many aspects of our lives. Suellen grew up in East Tennessee where she grew to love the mountains. Joyce grew up in West Tennessee where she loved the flat land and the Mississippi River. And now here we are living in Middle Tennessee where we have discovered the one thing we have in common is a keen sense of humor, and the grace to know a good story when we find one.

With all the media that swirl around us, iPads, URL's, iPhones, and who knows what other kinds of technology that has not yet been invented, the act of sharing a story orally with another human being, or in a room full of human beings is as old as language itself. Perhaps we are drawn to the human voice because it is one of the first things we hear in our mother's womb. It seems that we are built for hearing that voice with pleasant tones that rise and fall with expression. It is our first introduction to another person sometimes telling us what it means to be human

Storytellers use their voices and their bodies to create sounds and images in the minds of their listeners. Every storyteller has a personal way of telling a story so that it takes on the personal characteristics of that teller. Other people may tell the same story, but their tone of voice, their facial expressions, even the use of their hands will re-invent the story for the listener. Storytelling is more than entertainment. It is a way to transport listeners not only into a world of fantasy, but also into a world of sorrow, humor, beauty, or history. Storytelling is a way of bringing people together, to laugh, to cry, to become outraged, to learn personal history, and to think. And it can begin simply with the words, "I remember when."

A few years back both of us asked students to seek out the oldest member of their family or neighborhood available to them and listen to their story. Suellen asked her students to interview that person about important events in his or her life. Joyce asked her students to ask one simple question out of a list she provided. "What was the weather like on the day you were married?" Or "Where were you when you saw your first airplane?" Not a single student had to "develop" a story; the stories developed with the answers given. The questions elicited other questions which elicited more information. Each person who answered the question began to talk about their answers and went into detail.

Students shared with their classmates the stories they heard from the people they interviewed. They then thanked us for giving them that assignment. Not long after the storytelling class, one student called Joyce in tears. Her grandmother, whom she interviewed, had suffered a massive heart attack and had passed away. The student thanked Joyce for giving the assignment in class. Suellen had a similar experience when a student expressed her gratitude for the assignment. Her grandfather had passed away not too long after she had interviewed him, and she cherished having his voice on the recording she made during the interview, a priceless treasure. We hope that reading these stories will remind you of stories that people in your own family treasure; even better, we hope you will write down those stories for all to enjoy.

We want to capture the voices of our storytellers in this book with the hope that readers will read them aloud to friends and family. As good as they are on paper, these stories really only come alive when captured in the human voice involved in the "tellin'." Most of all, we hope you will hold some of them close to your heart and learn to tell them to your own family and friends.

Suellen Alfred

Joyce Tatum

Aunt Mollie's Leg

Joyce Milligan Tatum

I grew up in upper West Tennessee near Reelfoot Lake in a very small community called Mason Hall. The backyard of our house connected with the playground at my elementary School, so every day I would walk to school. That short walk proved to be my undoing on more than one occasion.

My fathers' younger sister was named Mollie. Aunt Mollie never married. She was what the family referred to as a "floater." She never learned to drive and lived with my grandfather until he passed away. Then she came to live with us for about two months. On a Sunday afternoon Daddy would take her for a ride over to Uncle Taylor's house.

In about eight weeks, Uncle Taylor would take her over to Uncle Bob's; and then she would go on to Aunt Effie's house and finally over to Aunt Bessie's before she would start the cycle all over again at our house.

I loved it when she was at our house. My Mother was a great cook, and her food was known far and wide; but her baking skills were another matter. However, Aunt Mollie could bake. Bread, biscuits, cakes, pies, brownies and cookies, she could do it all. Much to my Mother's irritation, I might add. Almost every afternoon when I would come home from school, Aunt Mollie would have something heavenly smelling in the oven.

My main reason though for loving Aunt Mollie so much, was for her prosthesis (her artificial leg). It was fantastic! She had lost her left leg from the knee down as a result of gangrene that she got from a blister on her heel when she was ten years old. After she turned eleven she got her artificial leg and every so many years after that, as she grew larger, a new leg had to be created.

I was six the year I started to first grade. Back then we didn't go to kindergarten, so first grade was my introduction to the public school system and to the teachers. A few days into the school year, Aunt Mollie arrived for her customary stay at our house. I was anxious to tell her all about school and how exciting it was, and she listened intently. She always did. That night she stayed up to unpack and get her room in order. When she went to bed she took her leg off and placed it beside the bed.

The next morning, seeing that she was still asleep when I got ready to leave for school, I decided to "borrow" her leg. What harm could it cause? It was "show and tell" day, the first one; and I wanted it to be special. I planned on sneaking the leg back home at recess time, and Aunt Mollie would never know it was missing.

I got an old potato sack from the shed, slipped her leg in it and trotted across the back yard to school. It was so neat! I was going to be the hit of Mrs. Velma Buckhanan's first grade classroom. Just before eight o'clock while Mrs. Buckhanan was out in the hall greeting the students, I knew I had to stash the leg until "show and tell" time. I dragged a chair over to the closet, climbed up on the chair and put that leg on the top shelf so that Mrs. Velma wouldn't find it. I closed the door and made the entire class, all ten of them, promise not to tell what was hidden it that closet.

We had been in class less than thirty minutes when the second grade teacher, Mrs. Opal, came in to borrow a box of safety scissors for a cutting project in her classroom. They were in that closet! When Mrs. Velma opened the closet door, Aunt Mollie's leg fell out. I still remember those screams, first Mrs. Opal, then Mrs. Velma, then the entire classroom. Now, if you have ever been around a bunch of first graders you know that if one screams, they all scream. I kept trying to hush them, but was having no luck.

Mr. Overall, the principal, who just happened to be in the hallway, rushed in and caught Mrs. Velma just as she fainted. As he laid her across the table in front of him, he saw the leg.

"What the …? Whose leg is this?" he shouted as he held it up.

All ten first graders pointed at me.

"Young lady," he bellowed, "Is this your leg?"

"Well, not exactly," I replied, "You see it belongs to my Aunt Mollie. She's a pirate, and she only has one eye, and she wears a patch, and she has a bird, and, and, and….."

Now Mr. Overall was a tall man; and, when he straightened up to his full height, I began to sense that I might be in trouble.

"Go get your brother," he commanded.

Ronnie was in the eighth grade, and when I knocked on his classroom door and said the principal wanted to see him, he gave me that look that meant "What did I do?" His friends began to snicker and whispered things like "Heh, heh, heh, Milligan's in trouble," "Hey what did you do?" and "Little sister had to come get you, huh?"

When we got out into the hallway, Ronnie whispered, "I better not be in trouble over something you did, understand?" I refused to look at him, but by the time we had arrived back at the first grade door, I was trembling.

Ronnie went in first.

"Son, do you know whose leg this is?" he asked.

Ronnie turned to look at me, trying to figure out how Aunt Mollie's leg ended up in the classroom unattached to Aunt Mollie. I just shrugged my shoulders. He turned back to Mr. Overall.

"That looks like my Aunt Mollie's leg," he answered.

"Is she a pirate?"

Ronnie looked back at me again with a shocked expression. Just once you would think he would cover for me, but …..

"No sir. She's just a plain old lady," he replied.

"Go back to your room, son. I'll take care of your sister," Mr. Overall said.

Ronnie turned to go and whispered to me, "Wait until Daddy gets a hold of you this time."

Mrs. Opal had to be helped out of the room. Mrs. Velma took the rest of the day off because she was so shook up, and I had to take Aunt Mollie's leg home.

When Daddy came home from work and heard what I had done, he went outside for a few minutes. I'll never know for sure, but I think he might have been laughing. When he came in, he sat down and motioned for me to come over by him. He picked me up and very gently, but firmly, told me to "Never, ever, ever take Aunt Mollie's leg without her permission." He sat me down, looked at my Mother and with a shrug of his shoulders told her, "It's going to be a long twelve years."

Aunt Polly Williams: the First Lady of the Cumberland River

Mark Dudney

(The following is an excerpt from a story by the same title that appeared in the Cookeville *Herald-Citizen*, October 12, 2008. It is used with permission from the author and from the newspaper.)

Aunt Polly Williams of Gainesboro became a legend in her own time during the upper Cumberland's post-bellum period. She wore men's clothes and a man's hat and smoked a long-stemmed corncob pipe.

The young girl destined to become Aunt Polly experienced a brief childhood. Born Mary Ann Christian Lock on May 5, 1839, Polly was reared on the Cumberland River. Jim Lock, her father, owned a farm and operated a ferry just opposite where the Roaring River drains into the Cumberland. At age thirteen she married her first husband, James Eaton, and gave birth to a child the next year. She bore Eaton nine children, several of whom did not survive infancy.

Eaton served as a Confederate officer during the Civil War. During his absence, some Union men appeared at Polly's door. She had some whiskey stored, which she was using to treat a sick and teething daughter. When they started for it, Polly grabbed her gun.

"The first one to touch that whiskey is my man," she warned.

"Why, we could shoot you," one of the men replied.

"You'd better be damned quick about it," she snapped back. Apparently, she convinced the soldiers that she meant business; and perhaps they concluded that tangling with her was more trouble than it was worth. The Union soldiers then left Polly and her whiskey alone.

Aunt Polly operated the Gainesboro Hotel, located on the North side of the town square. When in 1904, the hotel was destroyed in a fire that devastated part of Gainesboro, Polly immediately bought and began to run a second hotel on the opposite side of the square. A black man named Andy Gee operated her livery stable at this second hotel. In late 1908, he was charged with selling whiskey and sentenced to six months in jail. Evidently, several white men had persuaded Gee to sell the whiskey. When the sheriff refused to release him, Polly prepared a petition seeking executive clemency on Gee's behalf. She enlisted several prominent citizens as signatories including Cordell Hull[1] and John Gore[2], who were partners in a law firm there in Gainesboro. Polly then boarded a steamboat to Nashville and went straight to the top.

Governor Malcolm Patterson's secretary entered his office and announced, "Sir, there is a woman here who's smoking a pipe and wearing a man's hat. She says she wants to see you."

Patterson immediately replied, "Send Aunt Polly in." Polly was predictably blunt with the governor whom she addressed by his nickname.

"Ham, they've got my Negro, Andy, in jail and I want to get him out." Patterson asked what the charges were; Polly replied that Andy was charged with selling whiskey.

"Is he guilty?" asked the governor.

---

[1] Some years later, Cordell Hull would become Secretary of State under Franklin D. Roosevelt.

[2] John Gore went on to become a member of the U. S. District Court for the Middle District of Tennessee. For more about Judge Gore, see Michael Birdwell's "Moonshine in the Upper Cumberland."

"He's guilty as hell, but that's not the question," she shot back. "I can't run my business without him." Polly returned to Gainesboro with a full pardon for Andy Gee, signed by the governor.

Once, as she sat on the porch of her hotel, a stranger arrived in a wagon, obviously lost. Rain was falling heavily, and the unpaved streets were flowing with muddy water.

"Can you tell me how to get to Gainesboro?" the man asked.

Polly puffed on her pipe and replied, "Step-down off that wagon and you'll be up to your ass in it."

Aunt Lovey Learns to Drive

Livey Holman as told to Sandra Hope Smith

(This story took place in the 1920's)

When Redd and I got married, he was working at the lock, and we moved into the house that was built near the lake. Redd operated a lock on the Cumberland River in Clay County, Tennessee. Near our house was a ferry, and Redd would help take that ferry back and forth across the lake. Of course, I didn't work anywhere at the time: I just kept house. We lived close enough that Redd would walk from our house to the lock and back home again for dinner[3] at noon.

Now, our house was built near the lake up on tall poles so that the floor was off the ground, just in case the lake got up and flooded the area. Redd always parked the car under those poles that supported the house so that it was sort of like a garage like people have today.

One day I didn't have a lot to do, and I had been yearning to learn to drive. I had watched Redd, and I didn't think it looked too hard; so I decided that I could do it! I could teach myself to drive while Redd was at work, and I wouldn't tell him anything about it until I could surprise him with my new skill. I made my mind up that I would sneak out to the car and try my hand at it once Redd left for the ferry that very afternoon.

Everything went just like I had planned. I put the key in, like I had seen him do, and I started the car! I put it in gear (first gear, I remember), and I took off around the house real slow. I did just fine!

---

[3] In the South the noon meal is sometimes referred to as "dinner," and the evening meal is sometimes referred to as "supper."

I pulled the car back up under the house and got out and looked to make sure I had parked it in exactly the same spot where Redd had parked it before. After that, I went on into the kitchen to start Redd's dinner.

Redd came home for dinner, and I never said a word. I tried real hard not to let on that I had been up to something. Soon Redd finished eating and went back to work. I went out and tried it again! I drove the car around the house real easy and pulled up under those poles just like before.

That evening, Redd came home and didn't come right on into the house. I went out to check on him, and he was at the car doing something. I thought to myself, Oh no! But he just said something about a flat tire. He changed the tire with the spare that was in the trunk, and took the flat with him the next day to have it patched at the garage in town.

Well, the next day, while he was gone to work, I tried my hand at driving that little car again. (I was getting better and better, or at least I thought I was!) That night, Redd come home and said he couldn't believe it, but he thought that he noticed another flat tire on the car. Now, the first didn't alarm me. I couldn't imagine that I could have been responsible for the flats, but just maybe – I bit my tongue and didn't say a word! Redd changed that second flat with the tire he got fixed at the garage. He planned to carry the second flat and get it fixed the next day.

I was nervous about trying it again after the two flat tires, but I did it anyway! I was real proud 'cause I was changing those gears easier and faster and was able to get my speed up some, too. After I drove around the yard, parked the car, and checked the tires I was satisfied that everything was all right. I vowed right then and there that I wouldn't give up until I learned to drive as good as Redd.

Redd come on home for supper a little while later; and, sure enough, he found another flat tire! This one had a nail in it! After Redd found that nail, he came into the house and looked at me. Well, I just started to cry and tell him all about my sneaking to drive the car while he was at work. When I got the part about where I had been driving, Redd listened; and then he started to laugh and laugh! See, I didn't know it; but before we had got married, Redd had torn down an old chicken house out behind the main house; and my driving path went right through where that old chicken house had been. Redd explained that more than likely there were still several nails lying around on the ground, and I was just lucky enough to pick them up.

 After that, Redd took me out on Sunday afternoons and let me try my hand at driving. At first, I just drove on the back roads. After a while Redd decided that I was ready, and he let me drive out on the blacktop. It wasn't long before I went and took my driving test and got my license. Then you couldn't have tied me down. I drove pretty much anywhere I wanted to; I even drove to Nashville once to see a doctor. The only place he would not let me drive was through the yard where that old chicken house had been, but that was all right with me.

Tax Collectors and Sinners:
Moonshine in the Upper Cumberland

Michael Birdwell

(This story is based on a longer story that appeared in the Cookeville *Herald-Citizen* on October 11, 2012. It is used with permission from the *Herald-Citizen* and from Michael Birdwell.)

In the early part of the Twentieth Century, citizens from many walks of life in the Upper Cumberland mightily resented the federal tax on whiskey. Moonshine remained alive and well in the area, and it was not unusual for a judge to hear a case against a moonshiner who was not paying the tax, and then turn around and buy a pint from the man he just convicted. Here is part of Michael Birdwell's story.

Federal judge Bland Ballard earned a reputation of lenience concerning moonshiners. An indicted man form Cumberland County, Kentucky, stood before him accused of manufacturing untaxed liquor. The prosecutor demanded the maximum sentence, but Ballard disagreed. Finding the moonshiner guilty, Ballard sentenced him to sixty days in jail and levied a fine of $100.00. Appreciative, the convict exclaimed, "Judge, if I ever make any more moonshine whisky, I'll send you a keg of it." Several months later, Judge Ballard received a five gallon cask of "superior moonshine whisky" accompanied by a thank-you note from the lapsed distiller.

John J. Gore, a native of Jackson County and former law partner of Cordell Hull, was appointed the first federal judge in the newly created Middle Tennessee District in 1922 by President Warren G.

Harding. Though nation-wide prohibition was the law of the land, Gore received his whiskey from long-time friends and moonshiners. Judge Gore tended to show leniency to many illicit distillers who stood in before him.

Stories about Gore and his time on the federal bench dispensing justice to moonshiners are legion. One oft-repeated story concerns two different moonshiners who appeared before his bench on the same day. When the first man stood before him, Gore demanded that the bailiff present a sample of the accused's product. The judge took a mason jar and shook it, checking the bead of the whisky to determine its proof. He then poured out a thin line on desk, lit a match, and set it aflame. The alcohol burned with a bright blue flame. Gore announced that he could find no fault with the man or his product: he was simply trying to improve his economic prospects. He charged the man a small fine and sent him home with a warning. The other accused moonshiner stepped forward, and the same procedure ensued. When Gore set fire to the other man's whiskey, it created an orange flame. Gore turned red with rage announcing, "This man is a menace! He is manufacturing poison and is a threat to the community!" and then sentenced him to the maximum penalty available under the law.

On another occasion Gore visited a moonshiner on a snowy evening in the late 1920s. He purchased a couple of gallons of whiskey in individual pint jars. Arriving at his home as the snow piled up, he left the two gallons of hooch in a cardboard box on his back porch. The following morning Gore went out to retrieve some firewood and noticed that all of the jars had frozen and burst indicating that there was more water than alcohol in the whiskey. In a rage he called the Jackson County sheriff and demanded that he arrest the moonshiner. When [the moonshiner] appeared in court he was found guilty and sentenced to the maximum penalty.

During Prohibition, America's thirst created an enormous demand for white lightening, and Jackson County, Tennessee, was nationally known for the quality of its product. Today, the interest in legitimate moonshine sold in liquor stores and in boutique distilling shops is on the rise; and what was for decades Tennessee's number one industry may yet flourish again, as new distilleries such as Collier and McKee, Corsair, and Short Mountain join the ranks of Jack Daniel's and George Nickel.

The Art of Dumpstering

Heather Gothard

Heather Gothard

Author's Note: Small rural communities in Tennessee often consisted of a store, a school, a church, and a dumpster. All were gathering places for local residents. Sadly, these iconic symbols of small community living are rapidly becoming a memory of bygone days. The story below is the result of having lived in such a small rural community and regularly taking my trash to the dumpster.

The farmer stoops beside the dumpsters untying bags with tobacco-stained hands, face as furrowed as his fields. The bags have been left by people who discarded them at the dumpsters. He reaches into one of the bags and comes up with a ladle whose handle is bent in the middle. He runs his thumb around the inside of the bowl and puts it in his pocket. With what appears to be a keen sense of value and a poor sense of smell, he continues to reach in and sort the bag's contents. He occasionally mutters, "This'll work," as he adds some useful find to his collection of treasures in deep overall pockets.

The two dented and chipped green dumpsters with lids flung open sit bumped up against snarls of blooming ragwort, sumac, and fleabane just off the main road. A stenciled sign posted by the local authorities details what items may not be dumped such as stumps, building supplies, dead animals and tires. But locals know that taking garbage to the dumpster involves more than following these posted rules. It involves more than driving up, lugging the bag from your trunk to the steel edge and heaving it up and over. It requires knowledge of and adherence to proper rules of dumpster etiquette.

As I continue to observe the intricacies of dumpster behavior, these are the seven rules I am learning about my garbage:

1. Things that are smelly, mushy, or totally useless to anyone should go in a garbage bag tied in a very tight double knot to discourage anyone from untying it. It is optional to put things that are still edible in the gnarly pans on the ground for the cats.

2. Small things of questionable usage should go in garbage bags tied loosely and placed on top of other garbage, or if appropriate, draped tastefully over the side of the dumpster.

3. Large items of questionable usefulness should be placed outside the dumpster towards the rear so as not to be prominently placed but still readily visible.

4. Large items which are definitely useful should be placed outside the dumpster attractively displayed so that passers-by can easily determine if among them there is something they want.

5. Small sticks and scraps of wood which can serve as kindling are acceptable in the winter but not in the summer. Place in a pile toward the side.

6. Discarded clothes should be put in a bag by themselves. If they are great clothes, leave the bag loosely tied outside the dumpster toward the front. If there are only a few pieces, it is acceptable to drape them on the side if no rain is forecast. If they are badly worn or need repair, place a closed but untied bag in the dumpster on top. It is considered courteous to leave only seasonally appropriate clothing. Off-season items should go to your attic until the season is right to discard them.

7. Cardboard boxes can be stacked tidily towards the rear. Not for recycling, because the county doesn't, but so that you have something in which to cart off your finds, rather like Sam's Club.

I recently took an ancient, heavy, but still intact ironing board to the dumpster. As I was leaning its awkward bulk in an attractive position against the dumpster, a car drove up. The red-headed lady who feeds the dumpster cats got out with her two milk jugs of scraps. She slowed as she approached the ironing board.

"Throwin' that away?" She eyed the board.

"Yep. I got a new one. But it does seem a shame. It's really in good condition," I replied.

"Well, I'll take it," she said decisively. "Just put it in the back seat of my car."

I felt smug, like a salesperson closing a deal. Then I thought, I'm throwing this thing away. Why am **I** hauling this 30-pound monstrosity to **her** car? The rightness of it soon fell into place though; it was a swap for her kindness to the cats.

Last spring there was a console television with the screen smashed positioned in the "good stuff" place. The next time I passed, some of its inside parts were lying around the housing. And the next time, even more pieces were lying about. Soon little remained but the shell, which someone politely hoisted up for the dumpster to digest.

On another occasion, I took a door we had not used in the building of our house because it had a hole punched in the lower panel. I pondered its state of usability and finally decided to lean it up against the dumpster. Ten minutes later when I made my return pass, it was gone.

A point of caution when you arrive at your dumpster: make your presence known. My friend and neighbor tells of the time she tossed a bag into our local dumpster and heard a loud "ouch." Her bag had landed on a neighborhood treasure hunter. They exchanged apologies for hitting and for being in the way. This unfortunate encounter was a breach of dumpster etiquette, but quickly repaired with sincere apologies. Not as easily repaired was the time the green and pink vase discarded by Miss Effie Pearl Roach reappeared on her kitchen table with gladiolas as a neighborly offering to mourn her brother's untimely demise at 87.

Miss Effie Pearl, the tobacco farmer, and the redheaded lady who feeds the stray cats are all my neighbors. They have learned the fine art of give and take. I, myself, have not as yet taken anything from the dumpster; but when that day comes that I can both give and receive with the kindness and graciousness of these good folks, I will know I have truly become a part of my dumpster community in these Tennessee hills.

Bubba and Rumpelstiltskin

Suellen Alfred

Things were buzzing at Head Start today. The children were grinning from ear to ear as they filed in the classroom. They had been told that they were going to see a play that had been written just for them. The students in the drama class at the local high school had written a theater script based on the fairy tale, Rumpelstiltskin in which a malevolent elf refuses to return the queen's child until she can tell him his name.

Since there was no auditorium, all the children assembled in a large classroom that could accommodate all of them if they sat on the floor. The room was dark except for the portable theatre lights that illuminated the front of the room. The children settled down with wide-eyed attention. The head start teachers were a little surprised by how quiet and well-behaved they were. As the production proceeded, the tension mounted as the desperate young woman tried to guess Rumpelstiltskin's name. James, the high school student who portrayed Rumpelstiltskin, was doing a masterful job of building suspense every time he asked the Queen if she could tell him her name. Especially gratifying to the Head Start teachers was the fact that this actor grew up in the neighborhood where the Head Start program was located. He had shown remarkable talent for music and acting during his high school days, and he had "come back home" to share his talent with the children of his community, a number of whom knew him and his family. In fact, in that community, unbeknownst to his fellow actors, James went by the distinctly untheatrical nickname of "Bubba."

Among the children in the audience, the excitement continued to build as James portrayed Rumpelstiltskin, taunting the heroine with the very important question of his identity. The third time that James demonically delivered the line, "Do you know who I am?" The tension was apparently too great for one four-year old who lived in James' neighborhood. He jumped to his feet and shouted, "I know who you is. Your name is Bubba!'"

Chainsaw Nightmare

Roger Hyder

(This story originally appeared in *Teaching Through Stories: Yours, Mine, and Theirs. Norwood, Massachusetts: Christopher-Gordon, 1998.* It is used with permission from authors Betty Roe and Sandra H. Smith and from the author of the story, Roger Hyder.)

July 11, 1995, started out as most days had that summer. My daughter Tiffany and I loaded our saws and other supplies into our log truck and headed to the tornado-stricken area near City Lake. We were in good spirits as we traveled to our job site for a day of cutting trees that had been blown down by the tornado. We stopped at the service station to get gas for the truck and also to get our daily ration of beef jerky and cold drinks.

When we got to the woods, I began to cut trees into logs, while Tiffany began to drag the trees to the log yard. We were having a good time talking and working together, as we always do. I was cutting a tree that had a lot of pressure on it because it had been blown down. The limbs were kicking back as I cut them off, but I had everything under control – or so I thought.

Suddenly a limb that I was sawing broke loose, jerking my saw out of my hands. The limb came back, and I thought it hit my knee. When I looked down, my pants were ripped from the knee to the ankle. It was then that I realized the limb was not what had hit me. It was the chainsaw that had cut me while it was running wide open. The cut started on my knee cap and went to the back of my leg.

Just as I realized that my leg was cut, Tiffany saw what had happened and went for the truck to take me to the hospital. I did not know how fast I would lose blood and was afraid I might pass out. I desperately wanted to stay awake and help Tiffany stay calm. We could not tell how deep the saw had gone into my leg. All we could tell was that it had hit my kneecap. The cut was gaping open, and blood was running down my leg and into my boot. While Tiffany was getting the truck, which was parked several hundred yards from the log yard, I dragged myself to the log yard so she would have a place to turn around. She was fifteen years old and didn't have her license to drive. Before that day, she hadn't driven a big truck any place but in a field.

Tiffany came through the woods like a professional truck driver and helped me get into the truck. We headed to the hospital, which was about twenty minutes away. She had to drive through heavy traffic while I sat beside her bleeding and moaning and complaining about the slow traffic. She pulled up to the emergency entrance at the hospital and got a nurse to bring a wheel chair to take me into the emergency room.

Tiffany called my wife, Gail, and told her that there had been a slight accident and that we would be home in a little while. She assured Gail that she did not need to worry, that it was only a minor cut, because she didn't want to worry her mother until she actually knew the extent of the accident.

The doctor checked the cut and told us that I would need a bone specialist to repair the damage to my knee. He ordered x-rays because he could not tell if the bone was broken or how severe the damage to my knee was. He could feel saw tooth marks in the bone. After the x-rays had been developed, a bone specialist checked the x-rays and looked at my injury. She seemed to be in a good mood and told me that I was lucky that there were no broken bones or any permanent damage to my tendons or ligaments. She said that I should not lose much of my leg and announced that she would be back at 4:00 pm to sew it up. It was 11:00 am, and I was thinking that I would bleed to death by then.

The bleeding finally stopped, but the pain was beginning to come back, so I was admitted to the hospital and given some very strong pain medication. The pain medicine helped a little; and with my daughter encouraging me and telling me stories, I was able to rest until it was time for the doctor to sew up my leg.

When I was in the operating room and the surgeon sat down and started to hum, I knew that I was in good hands. The next thing I knew, I was in the recovery room; and Gail and Tiffany were there to greet me. The Surgeon had told Gail it would be a slow healing process because she had to remove some of the skin and flesh that the saw had damaged too badly for her to repair. The surgeon was optimistic about my recovery, saying that, although I would be in a great deal of pain for a few days, I would be up and around soon.

The next day, Gail loaded me up, equipped with crutches, and we headed for home. That was the longest trip I have ever made. Every bump felt like a knife sticking into my leg, and I was not a happy traveler.

The next eight days I spent in the house, not able to bend my leg or put any weight on it. The ninth day, I went back to the doctor who examined my leg and told me to bend it as much as possible so it would not form too much scar tissue. She also told me to quit using my crutches and walk as much as possible. I was able to go home and take a walk with my family to the end of the driveway. After that, my recovery was much faster, thanks to a good doctor and much help from my wife and daughter.

My knee is still numb, and it feels really weird when something touches it. When I go up or down steps or stand for a long period of time, it swells and hurts. Like a person who has arthritis, I can tell when the weather is going to change because my leg hurts. But I am thankful for a daughter who stayed cool during a crisis and a leg that is still attached to my body.

Hometown Characters

Joyce Milligan Tatum

Sometimes in life you meet some unique people who stick in your mind for years afterward. I think that over the years I have met more than my share of such people.

Mr. J.

He was a brilliant man, very intelligent, very smart in many ways, except when it came to hygiene. Mr. J taught at the university. He would put on one clean shirt each quarter and then wear the shirt for the entire quarter. Now does that sound normal? His car was a huge mound of papers and magazines that he was saving for who-knows-what. Whenever he traded cars he left all of the garbage in the old car and moved on to the next one. He never took anything from one vehicle to another. He just started another new heap. One day in midsummer as I was driving in town, I cut through his neighborhood. There he was mowing his grass in a Speedo and rubber boots. I was so surprised that I turned around and went back down the street just to have another look. I am sorry I did, because that picture still haunts me to this day.

Mr. B.

Another character who shaped my world was Mr. B who was a history teacher. I loved history and I loved Mr. B's classes. He thought that the CIA was looking for him. He knew too much history (or so he thought). He was always looking out the classroom window to see if anyone was watching him. He never left the building by the same door through which he had entered. Sometimes we would see him outside in his car looking out the car windows. He would look around carefully, back out of his parking place, drive around the parking lot, and finally park in a different spot. He said the CIA had bugged his parking spot.

Mrs. C.

Mrs. C. was a woman who had way too much time on her hands. She was married five times to four different men. She believed in recycling so she married one of the guys twice. Number one and number four were the same guy. She claimed that he was the love of her life. Ha! She suffered from delusions. After being married to the guy for a few weeks the second time, she began to think that he somehow had planted a chip in her brain that could read her mind. Never mind that the man had a tenth grade education and could not for the life of him put a simple puzzle together. He was so limited that "Old Maid" was a card game he could never get a grip on. This man had somehow gotten a microchip, read the directions, and while C. slept inserted the chip in her brain? Talk about being shy of a full load!

Jake Bridgewater and the Lawyer

Suellen Alfred

(This story originally appeared in *Teaching Through Stories: Yours, Mine, and Theirs.* Norwood, Massachusetts: Christopher-Gordon, 1998. It is used with permission from authors Betty Roe and Sandra H. Smith.)

Jake Bridgewater was an infamous schemer who had a farm in the community during the early part of the 20th century. He compensated for his lack of formal education by using clever, problem-solving common sense. He was also a skinflint of mythological proportions who hated to spend money as much as he liked to make it.

One day Jake had to go to court over a property dispute about a boundary line. The judge took only a few minutes to rule in Jake's favor. As Jake and his lawyer were leaving the court house Jake said, "Well, now, how much do I owe you for helping me out?"

"Fifty dollars," said the lawyer, with great self-assurance.

"Fifty dollars?!"Jake exclaimed, astonished. "Fer just ten minutes?"

"Jake, you're not payin' me for what I did. You're payin' me for what I know," said the lawyer in his well-pressed three piece suit. So Jake paid the lawyer with great reluctance, in cash, as Jake never used a bank account; and they both went on their way.

A few weeks later, on a back country road, Jake met the lawyer trying to persuade an uncooperative cow to cross a small bridge that spanned a noisy stream. "Jake, I can't seem to get this cow to cross this bridge. I'll pay you a little somethin' if you'll help me out," the lawyer said.

Without a word, Jake picked up a feed sack out of his wagon, placed it over the cow's head, and led her across that bridge as pretty as you please. The lawyer was visibly impressed and very relieved. "Well, thank you Jake," he said. "I never would've thought about using a tow sack. Now, how much do I owe you for helping me out?" (Anybody with a grain of imagination can predict the ensuing conversation, but for those who are still reading on the literal level, here is the rest of the story.)

"Fifty dollars," said Jake, with great self-assurance.

"Fifty dollars?!" exclaimed the lawyer, astonished. "For leading a cow across a bridge?"

"Mr. Lawyer, you ain't payin' me for what I did. You're payin' me for what I know," said Jake, in his rumpled overalls.

So the lawyer reluctantly paid Jake the fifty dollars, in cash, as Jake never used a bank account; and they both went on their way.

Jake Bridgewater and the Doctor

Randy Smith as told to Suellen Alfred

(This story originally appeared in *Teaching Through Stories: Yours, Mine, and Theirs*. Norwood, Massachusetts: Christopher-Gordon, 1998. It is used with permission from authors Betty Roe and Sandra H. Smith.)

Jake Bridgewater was a prosperous farmer who grew a bodacious lot of hay. People came from all over the county to buy it. One day Dr. Jones drove his wagon over to Jake Bridgewater's farm to buy some hay. Back in the spring, Dr. Jones had treated Jake for a broken arm, and the two men knew each other quite well. After Jake loaded the doctor's wagon with the hay, Dr. Jones said, "Thank you Jake. Now how much do I owe you for this hay?

Jake acted as if he had not even heard the doctor. Instead he asked, "Now how much do I owe you down to your office?"

"Twenty five dollars and seventeen cents," said the doctor. "How much do I owe you for the hay?" he repeated.

Jake looked up at the sky, scratched his chin, and narrowed his eyes in thought. "Well, I believe it comes to right at twenty five dollars and seventeen cents. Did you ever see anything come out so even?"

Jake Bridgewater and the Ice Box

Randy Smith as told to Suellen Alfred

(This story originally appeared in *Teaching Through Stories: Yours, Mine, and Theirs.* Norwood, Massachusetts: Christopher-Gordon, 1998. It is used with permission from authors Betty Roe and Sandra H. Smith.)

In the town where Jake Bridgewater lived, the proprietor of a local store ordered a large, fancy safe. When it came in by train, it was so heavy that it had to be offloaded by a crane which picked it up and drove it only a few blocks up the street to the store where it was to be installed. The store owner had built a flat bed with wheels. The plan was for the crane to lower the safe onto this mobile flat bed and roll it into the store.

For some reason, the crane began to malfunction. The driver could not get the safe to lower down to the flatbed. Nobody in that small town knew how to fix such a complicated piece of machinery, and calling someone in from the nearby city would cost an arm and a leg. So there the safe was, suspended in midair dangling just over the heads of men who had gathered around, as men will do, to talk about their dilemma.

In desperation, they contacted Jake Bridgewater who was known far and wide for his clever problem solving skills. After pondering for a while, Jake told the men to build a large box, a little bigger than the safe, and tall enough to reach it as it dangled in midair. The men built the box on top of the large mobile flatbed. After the box was built, they built a ladder alongside the box, so that a man could climb the ladder to reach the safe.

Jake sent the men in trucks over to the ice house to gather up as much ice as they possibly could. Fortunately they found enough to fill the box to the brim so that the ice was sitting just under the safe that dangled in the air. Jake climbed the ladder, unhitched the safe from the hook on the crane, and watched with great satisfaction as the safe settled softly on the ice. During that hot summer day, it did not take the ice long to melt and lower the safe to the bottom of the box where it settled on the flat bed and a group of hefty men rolled it into store where it still sits to this day, too heavy to move no matter who bought or sold the store.

Jake Bridgewater had saved the day.

Hoghead Williams Ain't Got No Sense

Randy Smith as told to Suellen Alfred

Hoghead's Disease

Hoghead Williams was walking down the street on a bright sunny day, when one of the townspeople stopped him and said, "Hello Hoghead. What are you doing home? I thought you had joined the army."

"Well, I did," says Hoghead, "but they sent me home."

"What for?"

"They said I had a disease."

"Why, you look healthy as a horse. What kind of disease did you have?

"They said I had illiteracy."

Hoghead's Engagement

Hoghead Williams had finally found himself a girlfriend who lived in a wide place in the road called Ottway. He became so fond of her he asked her to marry him. Unfortunately she did not have a very good reputation. When he told a friend about the upcoming wedding, the friend was upset that Hoghead would marry this particular woman. "Hoghead, I don't believe I'd marry that woman if I was you," he said.

"What for? "Asked Hoghead.

"Well, she's slept with everybody in Ottway!"

Hoghead scratched his head and pondered a minute.

"Well, Ottway ain't very big," he said.

Hoghead's Trick

One day Hoghead came in the barber shop with a paper sack in his hand. The barber and some of his customers had developed a silly game of guessing how many items were in a given sack. Hoghead had seen other people say to the barber, "If you can tell me how many apples are in this sack, I'll give you all of them." Hoping to get in on the fun, Hoghead walked up to the barber and said, "If you can tell me how many peaches are in this sack I'll give you both of them."

Lady Godiva (Southern Style)

Joyce Tatum

I grew up with four older brothers. There were three boys who lived next door on one side, and one boy on the other side. Across the road were two more boys. So you can see why I did not always act like a typical girl. My parents were thrilled when I was born, especially my Mother who had endured four boys and a husband with grace. She thought she now had that sweet, wonderful, dutiful daughter she had longed for. Oh, how wrong she was!

My hair was long – very long. Down to my knees long, and it was hot that summer. I hated my hair. My Mother would roll it at night so that I would have ringlets the next day, but before lunchtime it would be wild and wet and dirty. She would pull it back in a ponytail and sigh. Never mind ribbons, I could never keep them in my hair, nor barrettes. Trying to find them in the evening would be a waste of time and energy. Only very strong rubber bands would do.

One of my favorite pastimes was riding "Champ," the horse that belonged to the three boys next door. One very hot summer afternoon when I was five, I was riding Champ bareback around the field. The longer I rode the hotter I got. Nickie, who was close to my age, was under the tree trying to stay cool with a soft drink and a comic book. Nickie looked up and saw me wiping sweat from my around my neck.

"You should just ride naked like Lady Godiva," he said.

"Who?" I asked. "Who's that?"

"She was this lady who rode bareback on a horse so that people could have food."

Even though Nickie's grasp of history was not the greatest in the world, I thought for a minute or two; and seeing that it would be cooler to ride with no clothes on and that it just might solve world hunger, I figured I would give it a shot.

So off came the shorts and top and underwear. I was already barefoot. I had been riding like that for several minutes when two of my brothers, Ronnie and Jerry, opened the gate and came into the field.

Ronnie yelled out, "What are you doing? Get your clothes on before Mama sees you."

Now what happened next is one of those stories that has grown into a legend in the small town of Mason Hall. Every time someone reminisces about the incident, it changes. Some say that Nickie spooked Champ; others say that Champ had grown tired of going in circles and saw the open gate that my brothers had just come through; others say I made it happen. Everything happened so fast, that all I can say for sure is that I DID NOT MAKE IT HAPPEN.

Champ took off running for the open gate. Ronnie and Jerry were right behind him trying to catch him. If Champ had gone left I would have been OK since it leads into a big open field; but Champ went right, then took a hard right again toward the middle of Mason Hall.

Mason Hall was not a large community; only about 500 people lived there at the time. There was one gas station, two grocery stores, a diner, a bank and a cotton gin, all along the main road. This all happened on a Friday afternoon; and it seemed like everyone was there, grocery shopping, picking up something from the diner for Friday night dinner, cashing their checks, and getting gas for the weekend. Which was where my Father was, getting gas for the car, when I passed him riding bareback and bare naked on that horse.

Now granted, my long hair did cover me at times, but there was still nothing left for the imagination.

Ronnie and Jerry were running for all they were worth trying to stop Champ. They saw Daddy there at the gas station and knew when we all got home, it would not be pleasant.

Meanwhile back at the house, my Mother was setting the table for dinner when she got the first phone call.

"Mattie Lee, this is Velma. I just saw your youngest go by on that horse. Did you know she was naked?"

"What?" my Mama screamed. She dropped the phone and ran outside. Nickie was still under the tree reading his comic book.

"Where's Joyce?" she screamed at him.

Startled by my Mother's tone of voice, he dropped his book.

"She went that way," he pointed toward town, "but don't worry. Ronnie and Jerry are with her."

According to Nickie my Mother made some strange sounds as she took off toward the stores.

Meanwhile, Champ had grown tired of his run and stopped. He just stopped in the middle of the road. I almost went over his head. I had long ago dropped the reins and had been hanging on to his mane for dear life. My backside was red and raw from all the bouncing, and my hair was in so many knots that I knew it would take a long time to brush it out. My brothers came running up. Jerry jerked off his tee shirt and threw it at me while Ronnie grabbed the reins. I was shaking so bad that I reached for Jerry to get me off.

"No" said Jerry. "We are in enough trouble already. I'm not taking you off that horse so that you can show your rear end all over town."

Daddy saw Mama running toward town and opened the car door for her. They could see down the road that the boys had caught Champ, so they turned around and went home. The boys got me back home where we had some serious explaining to do to both Mama and Daddy.

I couldn't sit down for a week. Not because of a spanking that I should have gotten, but because horse hair itches on bare skin. I wasn't allowed to ride Champ for a long time, but at least one good thing came out of my adventure. Since my Mother became so impatient with all of the knots in my hair, I got my hair cut short!

Martha and the Wheat Field

Suellen Alfred

My friend Martha grew up on a farm where her father planted a large field of wheat. Martha loved the beauty of the wheat as it waved in the breeze almost like the ocean. She often wondered what it would feel like to "swim" into the middle of that wheat ocean. When she was finished "swimming" she could relax on the cool ground and watch the clouds go by.

One day she decided she would spend the afternoon doing just that. So she crept into the field and lay down, looking up at the clear blue sky. She began to make up stories; her imagination went wild. She pretended that she was a wounded soldier on the field of battle. Gosh, she thought, if I really were injured out in this field, no one would be able to find me because the wheat is taller than I am. So she thought about what she would do if she found herself in that predicament.

I know what I could do, she thought. I could roll around in the field and spell out the word HELP. Then if they sent out search planes, they would spot me from the air and send help. She completely forgot that if she were badly wounded, she would not be able to engage in such a rigorous process. So she rolled, and she rolled, and she rolled. Pretty soon she was finished, and she thought she had done a pretty good job of spelling out the word HELP. I wonder if a plane really could read my message she thought. Sure enough, a crop duster plane came flying over the field. It flew over slowly, and then it came back, flew over slowly again, and then came back, flew over a third time, but did NOT come back.

Pretty soon Martha heard all kinds of sirens and loud horns honking. The nearer they got the more she realized that they were coming to her house. It did not take her long to figure out that the pilot of that plan had told the Emergency Medical Technicians that somebody needed help over at the Bulow farm. She knew she was in trouble.

Now on the edges of many fields you will find drainage ditches that capture run-off water. Martha figured if she could crawl away from the HELP sign she had made, she could get to a drainage ditch and hide out until all the commotion was over. She crawled and she crawled moving carefully so as not to shake the wheat. So far so good, she thought. If she was lucky, she might even be able to climb out of that ditch and run to the house without being seen.

It seemed like an eternity to get to that ditch. She crawled and she crawled, taking care not to disturb those plants —or so she thought. She crawled and she crawled as she heard the search party looking for her, calling her name. She crawled and she crawled until she got to that drainage ditch. Finally she made it. Safe at last. No one had seen her. And once she was there, she decided to crawl out of the ditch and run to the house without being seen.

As she came up out of that ditch, the first thing she saw on the ground above her was not a pretty sight. It was her father's shoes! When she summoned the courage to look up into his face, she saw that her father was very, very angry. But the only thing he said to her in a booming angry voice was, "Go to the house." And she did.

I Know How to Drive

Suellen Alfred

My mother, Freeda Murray Alfred, grew up in Wells Springs, just outside Lafollette, Tennessee on a very large farm owned by her grandmother and assorted uncles. One cousin was a judge, one was a doctor, one was a representative to Congress, and mother's father was her fourth grade teacher. So you can imagine that education was valued highly in that family.

Although education was important, the folks in that area used terms and pronunciations that are no longer used today, when the family named my mother, they misspelled the name; and she spent her whole life telling people that her name was spelled "Freeda," not "Frieda," as it was usually spelled.

 Also, the people in Wells Springs used the term "school house" instead of merely "school." I remember mother using that term along with "dwelling house," "church house," "smoke house," and, of course, "out house." It appears that in that area in the early part of the 20th century, the word "house" was a much more generic term for a building. So it was important to add the appropriate adjective to specify the exact "house" to which one was referring. Nowadays, few people have smoke houses or out houses, so the word "house" seems to have taken on a more narrow implication as a synonym for "home" where one "dwells."

We had some pronunciation challenges when I was growing up. Although my mother's name was Freed**a,** in Campbell County where she grew up, her family called her Freed**ie**. That seemed to be the way they pronounced any name that ended in a long "A" sound. My grandmother's name was Nora, and one of my cousins was named after her. But they pronounced the name "Norie." Mother's older sister, Leoda, was called Leodie. These names never changed throughout my childhood, and I always had a hard time talking about these relatives around people who spoke standard English because it was hard to remember to pronounce their names correctly, the way standard English users would have me pronounce them. Doing so always made me feel like I had got too good for my raisin'.

The name of Mother's Congressman was J. Will Taylor. He was her first cousin twice removed. One time when J. Will Taylor left Washington on the train to come home to La Follette, mother's father, William Lawrence Murray, drove to Knoxville to pick him up at the train station. Now both men were well acquainted with John Barleycorn, and they had one too many drinks on the way home. By the time they got to Will Murray's house, it was almost dark; but it was clear from the scent of their breath and their weaving bodies that they were drunk. When Will Murray's wife, my grandmother, Norie Claiborne Murray, came to the door, she was very angry to find him and the Congressman in such a condition.

"You both are drunk. I'll not have two no-good drunk men coming in my house," she said. "You can just sleep it off out on the porch!" Now can you imagine treating a member of Congress so disrespectfully? Apparently, to Norie Claiborne Murray, no matter who he was, she was not going to allow any drunken person in her house. I don't know whether those men slept out on the porch or whether they drove to J. Will Taylor's house to sleep. Suffice it to say, my grandmother was the kind of person who would hold her ground no matter who you were.

Perhaps that is where Mother's sister, Myrtle Eve Murray Jones, got her rebellious nature. In the community where Myrtle and Freedie grew up, there was a young woman, Dorothy May, who had borne a child out of wedlock. (Dorothy May is not her real name. I have changed her name to respect her privacy.) In those days early in the 20th century, a girl who had a child out of wedlock had committed a terrible sin, and she was cruelly shunned by everyone in the community. Young girls were supposed to stay away from such women; so poor old Dorothy May was an outcast – but not to Myrtle Murray.

One time Myrtle and some of her friends skipped school; and when officials went to find her, there she was at Dorothy May's house. No doubt their grandmother, strait laced Rachael Rogers Claiborne, was scandalized. Mom said that Myrtle and her friends were brought back to the school house and made to sit on stools in front of the room with dunce caps on their heads and signs hanging around their necks on which was printed one phrase: "The Runaways."

Myrtle was an adventurous sort. When Freedie and Myrtle were in their early teens, one of their male friends took them for a ride in his new convertible, a treat beyond description for them, no doubt. Myrtle talked him into letting her drive. Now, Myrtle could no more drive a car than the man in the moon. So it didn't take long for the car to wind up in the ditch, with all three passengers sprawled out on the grass. Myrtle got up, frantically came over to Mom and shouted, "Freedie, are you hurt?"

"I can't get up," Freedie said.

"Oh. We need to get you to a doctor!" Myrtle said.

"Well, I am not hurt, but I cannot get up until you take your foot off my dress."

I never learned the name of that poor guy nor the condition of his car after Myrtle wrecked it, but I bet he never let Myrtle Murray anywhere near that car after that fiasco.

Speaking of driving, in traffic Myrtle was not one to brook fools lightly. When she was an adult, she lived in Indianapolis, Indiana.

According to a cousin, one time when she was in the middle of busy Indianapolis traffic, a fellow was following too closely behind her. At each red light he would honk the horn until the light turned green. This annoying behavior went on for several blocks. Of course Myrtle could not let this kind of horn harassment go. At the next light, while it was still red, Myrtle calmly got out of her car, walked back to the honker's car, reached into his car, removed his keys, disposed of them in the storm drain, and drove away as the light turned green. Nobody seems to know how she got away with that!

In another driving calamity, during World War II, when Myrtle's husband was stationed in the Army in Europe, Myrtle applied for a job at a manufacturing plant in Knoxville. The man who interviewed her asked, "Do you know how to drive a forklift."

"Sure," said Myrtle.

It did not take long for the boss to realize that Myrtle knew absolutely nothing about driving a forklift. The first time she made the effort, she plowed into a pile of boxes and scattered them everywhere. Of course she got fired for that little incident, but you can't blame her for trying.

On the Other Hand

Suellen Alfred

When I was a young woman, I attended Carson Newman College (Now Carson-Newman University) in Jefferson City, Tennessee. In fact, I graduated from that school over 50 years ago. Now this was a Southern Baptist College, and in those days the rules about dating were very strict. On one occasion we got a memo from the Dean of Students telling us that we women were lingering too long at the door of our dorms after coming in from our dates. In response to this edict against lingering, a group of us got together and marched en masse to the front of Butler Hall, a women's dorm, singing to the tops of our voices the hymn "I Am Resolved": "I am resolved no longer to LINGER, charmed by the world's delights. Things that are higher, things that are nobler, these have allured my sight."[4] Of course we sang the word "linger" even louder. We were too clever by half.

But first let me explain how dorms were set up in those days. As you entered the front door of Henderson Hall, the dorm where I lived, you found yourself in a large entrance hall. You saw a staircase in front of you. And to the left was the apartment of the housemother, who supervised the girls, making sure they came in at night before curfew, and reminding them frequently of the rules. We were not allowed to wear pants. We had to be in our rooms by 10:00 pm each night. See? I told you the rules were strict.

Across the hall from the housemother's apartment was a room that we called the parlor. It was a large room with couches and chairs

---

[4] Palmer Hartsough and James H. Fillmore, 1896.

where students could sit and study or visit with friends. Boys were not allowed in any part of the dorm except this parlor.

The housemother in my dorm was a very large woman who never smiled except in a facetious way when she was reminding us that we had broken a rule. She was judgmental and critical. She was supercilious in the extreme. We called her the Water Buffalo.

I remember one morning I was on my way to class, coming down from my room on the second floor. It was a bright cheery day, and I was whistling as I came down the stairs. Just as I got about half way down the stairs, here came the Water Buffalo, out of her apartment. "Sue Alfred, stop that whistling at once! Polite young ladies do not whistle." I was so stunned I **did** stop whistling – until I got outside, where I whistled one happy tune after another, all the way to class. But I think she is right, I never have in all my days heard a lady whistle.

So, one day in this parlor, two of my friends, Bill and Jeanette, were sitting on the couch. You can imagine that their relationship was a pretty serious one when I tell you that they got married right after they graduated from college. So, as all devoted couples do, they were casually sitting on the couch in the parlor enjoying a pleasant conversation. Bill was nonchalantly holding Jeanette's left hand in his right hand. Suddenly in came the Water Buffalo. She was very unhappy to see this young couple sitting so close to each other holding hands. As I said, she was a stickler for the rules. She thought sitting close together holding hands was an "inappropriate public display of affection." "Young man," she said sternly, "what are you saving for marriage?"

And Bill said, "The other hand."

Pay It Forward

Joyce Tatum

April was one of those months that was undecided that year. First warm, then cool, never constant. We had had some very warm days that week. Then during the night everything cooled down. That Thursday dawned bright, beautiful and cool. It was one of those days that made you want more. A brilliant blue sky, no clouds to be seen, everything bright and green. I had been working outside in my garden, and suddenly remembered that I had to go to the grocery store. I delayed it as long as possible – grocery shopping was not something I liked to do; so I finished the unhappy chore in record time, wanting to get home and have dinner ready for my husband when he got home.

As I was leaving the store, there she stood. Small, petite really, just a slip of a girl with long hair and glasses and carrying a backpack almost as big as she was. Our eyes met, and I could see that she was trying hard not to cry.

"Are you O.K.?" I asked.

In a small voice, not much above a whisper she replied, "Yes. May I have fifty cents, please?"

I stopped and pulled out my wallet. I found the two quarters and handed them over.

"It's your lucky day," I said. "I don't often have change"

She reached for the money and said ever so softly, "Thank you."

I smiled at her, gathered my bags together and went out the door. Any other time that would have been the end of the story, but not today. Just as I was closing the back end of the SUV, she appeared at my side.

"Could you take me to Wal-Mart, please?" she asked. I hesitated a little too long. "Someone was supposed to meet me here, but I've been here over an hour and they never showed up. I have a friend who works at Wal-Mart and she gets off in a half-hour and can take me home."

She slowed down her speech, "I guess I could walk there."

I looked at my watch and then at her. Something about her, something I'm not quite sure what, told me to reach out to her.

"Where's home? Where do you live?" I asked.

"Way out by Hidden Hollow. It's too far to ask you to take me there."

"Get in." I replied.

"My friend said she could help me out a little," the girl said.

"What is your name?" I asked her.

"Marsha," she answered as she fastened her seat belt. She was trying hard not to cry. Her lower lip quivered.

"How is your friend going to help you out?" I asked.

"My husband was in a car accident and totaled our car. He's out of work right now and we don't have any money. A friend was supposed to meet me at Kroger and help me buy some diapers and food. They never showed up," she sighed and a tear rolled down her cheek.

"You have a baby?" I asked.

"I have three children, all boys. A ten year old, a seven year old and a seven month old," she replied softly.

"My goodness! You have your hands full." I said.

"The boys are in school right now," she said "They'll be out soon for the summer."

"Where do they go to school?" I asked.

"Northeast," was her answer.

We pulled into Wal-Mart parking lot. Was it the way she looked, her answers, or her single tear that pulled at my heart? I'll never know for sure, but I do know that God whispered in my ear then and simply said, "Do it for me."

"Have you ever heard the expression, pay it forward?" I asked her.

"Yes" she replied.

I reached for my billfold and pulled out $50.00. I reached for her hand and pressed the money into her palm.

"Someday when you are able to help someone else, think of me, would you?" I asked.

"Are you sure?" she said as she looked at the money I had placed in her hand. "You don't even know me."

"Yes I do," I answered. "Your name is Marsha, and someday you are going to help someone and think of me. God bless you, Marsha."

She reached out and hugged me tight. "I'll do it for you someday. I promise," she said. She got out of the car, took a few steps, turned and waved. It was the last I ever saw of her.

A Personal Encounter with Mount St. Helens

Brice Stevens

Linda rousted us out before seven o'clock. Amidst our sleepy protests she announced, "It's my van, and I'm leaving. If you want to ride out of here, get up and pack."

"Linda, why are you so set on leaving right now?" I asked. "It's a beautiful morning!"

"I just want to go. Now. I don't know why," she said. She was so insistent, so full of fear that we finally agreed to do what she asked of us.

Soon we were on the road. We all relaxed and enjoyed the scenery as we traveled the twenty-some miles of forest and logging roads from our campsite back to the highway. Tall trees and occasional small ponds lined most of the road, broken here and there by clear cuts which revealed panoramas of western Washington's mountain crests receding to the misty blue horizon.

When we reached the highway an hour later, we all piled out, thankful for the chance to stretch. Looking up, we saw a black cloud rolling in across the western sky. We were surprised to see a small airplane that seemed barely able to outrun the cloud's leading edge.

"I haven't seen a storm come in like that since I was a kid in Indiana," I remarked.

"Looks like we're really in for it," a friend agreed.

A rabbit darted out of the undergrowth into the highway, paused with a look of surprise and confusion, then leapt into the brush across the road. A flicker flew from a high limb to the brush as if in pursuit of the rabbit. A pea green forest vehicle raced past us at breakneck speed.

"I wonder what his big hurry is," Linda said.

"I don't know," I said, "but that storm is nearly over us. We'd better get in the van or we're going to get soaked."

We were barely situated in the van when the storm of hail hit. Solid chunks clattered against the roof of the car and bounced off the road, accumulating to an inch deep in under a minute. Mike started the engine and pulled onto the highway, when the nature of the downpour abruptly changed. Large globules of mud suddenly coated everything, almost totally eliminating visibility. This lasted for only a minute or so in real time; much longer in the confusion of the crisis, as Mike slowed to a crawl. He pulled the washer fluid knob on the dashboard in an effort to keep the windshield clear enough to see through.

The mud fall ceased with the same suddenness that it started, and blackness enveloped us. We all rode in grim silence, unsure and disoriented by the unnatural phenomenon. I noticed that Linda's olive Native American complexion was nearly as pale as the rest of us were naturally. My wife Trinda's eyes were wide with wonder and fear. Mike's muscles were taught, his knuckles white from gripping the steering wheel. We looked at one another with mute incomprehension. I felt a welling panic.

The black gloom thickened. Visibility with the headlights dropped to a scant yard. We began choking on fine dust that poured in through the weary joints of the aging Volkswagen.

"The volcano," Trinda murmured.

"I think we are in trouble," Linda said with a trembling sigh.

Thoughts of Pompeii came to my mind. The volcano, of course. We had gone camping in the hopes of seeing the steam plume St. Helens had been producing for several weeks. And now the mountain itself was raining down on us. I kept imagining those Pompeii victims, choked and fossilized in their efforts to escape that ancient eruption.

We spoke very little. Linda summed it up. "I'm scared. I want out of here."

Ash fell. We slowly pushed on. I realized that it was not hail that hit us but probably a shower of pumice pebbles that first fell on us. There was no way to guess how much ash might fall on us or how far we would manage to travel before it forced us to stop.

I suggested trying to get to a twenty-four hour restaurant in Randle, about six miles down the road. "At least we'll be with other people, and they'll try to dig out a place like that before they go after isolated vehicles like ours," I said.

The others readily agreed. Having a goal that was within reach lifted our spirits. Unless the showering ash increased dramatically, we would be able to reach Randle before the highway became impassible.

In order to fight against the choking, stinging ash, Trinda collected everyone's bandanas. She opened the ice chest, soaked the bandanas in the melted water and passed them around. Tying them over our mouths and noses helped our breathing, but it could not keep the scratchy grit from our eyes.

Our progress was reduced by now to about three miles an hour. The road had disappeared under the thick layer of ash. The only way Mike could find our path was to listen for the gentle bumps of the road turtles marking the highway lanes; but he frequently lost the reassuring thump of the markers, and the crunch of gravel warned him he had strayed too far to the left or right. Mike had always seemed carefree, content to let others worry about responsibilities. But now, groping for a safe path out of the oblivion, his apparent calm as he finessed his way down the highway was belied by the iron determination that sculpted his face.

Suddenly our whole field of vision opened when a thick rope of lightning exploded across the highway at tree-top level. We gasped in horror as the ancient fir burst into flame, almost immediately extinguished by the heavy ash fall. For the next hour, this freakish staccato accompanied our trek. In the limited range of our headlights a bird dropped dead on the road. We saw the death dances of bees and insects etched upon the ash. The suffocating atmosphere, choking out fire and life became my greatest concern as we struggled ahead in grim silence. Was it the thick ash, or was a lack of oxygen from the volcanic gases that allowed nothing to survive but the frightening sulfurous bolts of lightning?

I studied my companions. Other than their pallor which I attributed to awe and fear, they seemed fine. Everyone's eyes were wide open and alert; no sign of drowsiness or disorientation. It must have been the thick ash outside the van, and not the air itself causing the bizarre events we were witnessing.

After two hours of work, no less grueling for us three passengers than for our driver, we felt more than saw openness around us. The hellish bolts ceased. The black seemed less pressing.

"It's not as bad here," Linda observed.

"I think we may be in Randle," I said. "Watch for a big driveway; that should be the restaurant."

"I think you're right," Mike told us. "We've come almost seven miles."

"Is that a sign post?" asked Linda, pointing to a dim silhouette that looked like a telephone pole set in a low rectangular planter.

"Let's find out," said Mike.

He pulled into a broad paved area and crept across it at a right angle from the highway. A brick wall materialized before us. We perceived a dim, steady light showing through the window.

"Let's see if they're open," Linda and Trina cried out together.

We all piled out of the old van and felt along the wall until we located the door. To our relief, it opened. Entering, we noticed only two customers, gray with ash, and a waitress seated behind the counter. Two kerosene lanterns provided illumination.

"Come on in," the waitress called cheerfully, "and close the door. We're trying to our best to keep the dust out of here." She drew four glasses of fresh cold water and hurried toward us with them.

"Here you go. You'll want to wash that dust out of your throats. The washrooms are right over there. Get yourselves cleaned up and come join our party."

We glanced at each other and broke into laughter. Largely it was the release from hours of stress and uncertainty that fueled our laughs. But the sight of ourselves uniformly dressed in gray ash from head to toe was compelling. Linda's thick black braids and Trinda's golden curls were identically gray. The only colors distinguishable were in our eyes, which were lattices of red and white from the irritating ash surrounding the colors of our irises. The other two patrons wore that same gray fashion we did, but they enjoyed the luxury of clean hands and faces.

We headed for the restrooms, eager to wash off the grime. Cool water never felt so good, stripping the tiny, glassy bits of ash off our skin and out of our eyes. We grabbed handfuls of tissues and blew more ash from our noses.

When we reassembled in the in the dining room, the waitress told us she could make cold sandwiches, but no hot food, explaining that the restaurant had lost its power during the first earthquake accompanying St. Helens' explosive eruption. Now that we were seated in a less mobile environment, we noticed the mild shaking of the continuing earthquakes. Thanks to Linda's uncanny sensitivity we had been traveling gravel roads when the eruption occurred, and we did not feel it. Nor had we heard the explosion. We learned later that the blast had been heard scores of miles away. Although we were fairly close to the event, we were in a valley over which the sound had skipped, as if in an eddy unaffected by the currents of a wild river.

We left the restaurant a couple of hours later when the ash fall had nearly stopped in our area. The black cloud still let no sunlight through. With the failed electrical system, the land was strangely dark. Our headlights were more effective now, beaming through the air that was no longer choked with ash fall; and we made good time. We were astonished by the number of birds and insects lying dead in the road.

Some twenty miles down the road, the dark cloud lightened to the same gray that shrouded the fields and buildings we passed. Soon we emerged from it into a brilliant landscape of blue and green. Here the state police had set up a road block. As they inquired about conditions along the highway we learned we were the first people to emerge from the devastation.

Having satisfied their curiosity, we found a place to park. We joined a crowd of people standing in clusters in a field and watched the continuing eruption. Watching the tremendous column of ash boiling from the mountains, we noticed that we, too, were the subject of curious glances and comments. At that moment we were all very glad we had heeded Linda's intuition and left the campsite that surely would have been the place of our death had we stayed there.

Surprising News

Posey Young

(The following narrative is based on *Posey Young: A Historical Video of Clay County, the Way we Lived: The Posey Young Story*. It is used with permission from Doug Young, who interviewed Posey for the video.)

Howard Reeves 'Posey' Young was born in Clay County, Tennessee, at Butlers landing in August 1930. He died in 2013. In the 1950's he served in the Marine Corps during the Korean War with J. D. Shell, who was from Signal Mountain. In the vast army of men from all over the United States, Posey and J. D., two Tennessee hillbillies, naturally gravitated to each other and became close friends. During one brutal battle, J. D. was badly wounded and put on a hospital ship bound for the United States. Posey's account of reuniting with his friend is compelling.

> About two months later [after J. D. left the battle field] it got back to me that he didn't make it. And that was in early '53, so I've lived with it all these years. I talked to my family and told them a little about it.
>
> I come in one evening and my wife said "You've got a big brown envelope in there." So I opened it up and there was mine and his [J. D.'s] picture . . . and down at the bottom there was his name, phone number, and address; so I told her, I said, "There's something wrong, somebody's pulling my leg. He died in early '52."

So I got nervous; I got shook up. She tried to get me to go to the hospital and get me a shot to calm me down, and I wouldn't go. . . .

She said "You gonna call the number?"

And I said "No, there's something wrong; it ain't right." But finally I took a couple of aspirins or so and I finally called.

Some lady answered the phone. I said, "Lady, who am I speaking to? "

And she talked very nice. "Who do you wish to speak to?"

I said, "Well I'd like to speak to an ex-marine." She screamed. You could hear her from here to way out in the road.

She said, "Is this you, Mr. Young?"

I said, "Yea."

She said, "Wait a minute. I'll get him."

So he gets on the phone and he said, "Young is this you?"

I said, "Yea; is this you J.D.?"

He said, "Yea."

Well, he couldn't talk; I couldn't talk. We didn't talk. We sat there and grunted around. I give him my phone number. I had his.

I said, "I'll call you in a day or two." Well, I hung up, and I didn't know what to think. I said, "He may not have no legs, he may not have no arms, he may not have nothing. I don't know."

So it really, really, really bugged me. So a day or two later we talked again. Every time we'd carry on a conversation we'd get a little looser. I'd get a little looser he'd get a little looser, so finally I said "J. D., I know you had bad luck."

"Well," he said "Yea, I got shot 16 times. The last two years of my military service I stayed in a military hospital in Memphis."

 He told me that his daughter had found my address through her work with the federal government. So we kept getting a little looser all the time. So one day I told him, "I want to come to see you."

He said, "I want you to." Well, during that time I had sent him a picture of me and my wife, so he told me on the phone. "I don't believe I'd a known you. You've got grey headed." So I didn't say much about that.

I took off down there . . . and on the way down there I got nervous again, cause you remember back in those days was when that Floyd [Forest] Gump picture came out with [the] Lieutenant [and] Da Nang and all that. [Here Posey is referring to a character who has lost both his legs in the movie *Forest Gump*.] I got to studying, I don't know what all I'm gonna run into. We got down there, and I pulled into the wrong drive way. Here come a big ole tall grey-headed man a limping over through there, so I rolled my window down.

He said "Young, is this you? I'm J. D.," and I said "J. D. you've got grey headed. I don't b'lieve I'd a known you if you hadn't told me who you was."

When Posey was hospitalized with heart trouble, J. D. came to see him in Erlanger Hospital. Ever since that first encounter they kept in touch until Posey died in 2013 at the age of 83.

The Trick that Worked

Jane Crooks as Told to Suellen Alfred

He had always been a trickster up to some kind of foolishness. But he had such an innocent face, people fell for his shenanigans nearly every time. He would pull your leg, even under the most serious circumstances, even when he got engaged to Cora and took her home to meet Aunt Lyla, the family matriarch. Not a single young person in Merle's family ever went to college or took a job or got married, or made any other serious decision without talking it over with this formidable lady. She was well-loved, authoritative, overbearing, and wise. And it didn't hurt that she had saved up a right healthy sum of money with no offspring to leave it to. But none of that kept Merle from having some fun, because he knew that under her crusty exterior, Aunt Lyla had a sense of humor.

When it came time to introduce Cora to the family, Aunt Lyla would be the first to meet this lovely girl who had said "yes"; and Merle wanted these two very special women to become good friends. "Now Cora, I think you will like Aunt Lyla," he said. "But there's just one problem."

"What is that?" asked Cora. *The old woman is probably going to be very difficult, and Merle is going to tell me that I have to watch my p's and q's,* she thought.

"Well, Aunt Lyla is a fine woman. But she is very hard of hearing. And she refuses to admit it. Won't wear a hearing aid. Doesn't want anyone to know that she can't hear it thunder. We will have to talk just as loud as we can, and pretend that nothing is wrong. So when I introduce you, be sure to speak up as much as you can."

"I think I can do that," said Cora. She did not notice the slight smile that came over Merle's face as he shared this important piece of information. She was simply relieved that the problem was not anything worse.

That evening, Merle called Aunt Lyla to tell her that he was going to bring his fiancée home to meet the family. "Now Aunt Lyla," he said, "Cora is a fine woman. But she is very hard of hearing. And she refuses to admit it. Won't wear a hearing aid. Doesn't want anyone to know she can't hear it thunder. I just talk as loud as I can, and pretend that nothing is wrong. So when I introduce her, be sure to speak up as much as you can."

"Poor child," said Aunt Lyla, who felt grateful that with advancing age she herself had been spared the kind of hearing impairment that afflicted so many of her contemporaries. She felt sorry that Merle's sweetheart should have to struggle with such a handicap at such a young age.

Soon the day arrived. Merle brought Cora home to meet the family. And he upheld the old tradition of making sure that Aunt Lyla was the first member of the family to meet his beautiful fiancée.

"Aunt Lyla," he shouted, "this is Cora Matthews. Cora, this is my aunt, Miss Lyla Womack."

Mercy, thought Aunt Lyla. She must really have a hearing problem.

Heavens, thought Cora. She must really have a hearing problem.

Neither woman had ever heard Merle speak so loudly before. And, eager to make a good impression and to communicate with this new person, each woman did as she was advised to do. She spoke at a very high volume.

"I am very pleased to meet you, young woman," shouted Lyla.

"I am very pleased to meet you, too, Miss Womack," shouted Cora.

"Won't you sit down and have a cup of tea?" asked Aunt Lyla. Her voice was loud and strong.

And so the conversation went, each woman shouting politely to the other. They were so intent on making themselves heard that they did not notice the grin that began to spread across Merle's face. It began with a slight smile that rapidly grew wider and wider. No one knows how long the two women would have gone on like that, shouting at each other, as they were cautioned to do; but soon they were mercifully interrupted by an enormous explosion of laughter. Unable to contain himself one minute longer, Merle had completely lost control. Both women were shocked that Merle who had always been such a sensitive man would laugh so disrespectfully and so uproariously at someone with such a handicap.

"Merle! I have never known you to be so rude!" exclaimed Aunt Lyla.

"I can't help it," he said, hardly able to get his breath. "I cannot keep a straight face any longer," he said. "Aunt Lyla, Cora is not hard of hearing. Cora, Aunt Lyla can hear now as well as she could twenty years ago. I told each of you that the other woman was hard of hearing just to get a big laugh. And I was not disappointed. It was hilarious just to sit here and watch two perfectly able women yelling their heads off at each other for no reason at all."

"Well! How could you play such a mean trick on such a nice person?" huffed Cora and Aunt Lyla in a unified reaction of embarrassment and disgust. And then they, too, broke into great explosions of laughter that was even heartier than Merle's.

The women took an instant liking to one another. Now, these two strangers had something in common that created a bond between them. They had been duped by a gentle trickster whom they both loved in spite of himself. The trick had worked.

Merle and Cora got married. Cora and Lyla remained good friends all the days of their lives. Neither of them ever fell for any more of Merle's tricks, and neither woman ever shouted at the other one again.

75

Uncle Bob's Lie

Tammy Davis Robbins

(This story originally appeared in *Once upon a Times*, Fall 1993, the storytelling newsletter for International Reading Association.)

There was a time not so long ago when the town of Celina, Tennessee prospered. Those were the days of the river raftsmen, strong men who floated logs down the Obey and Cumberland Rivers. Even though this time is long gone, Uncle Bob Riley, the most notorious of these raftsmen, had a reputation for telling the most outlandish lies in the county – and sometimes people even believed him. Stories about him are still passed down from one generation to another by the residents of Celina.

It was late in the evening, and Uncle Bob Riley, having worked all day, was eager to get home to hoe his corn. He was walking by a rather large house in front of which stood several men. When they saw Uncle Bob they walked to the road to greet him.

"Hey, Uncle Bob!" shouted one man

"How ya doin', Bob," asked another.

Well, I'm just fine, boys. And y'all?" came the reply.

"We're just fine," came the collective response.

"Uncle Bob," said one of the men. "Stop just a minute and tell us one o' yer biggest and best lies."

"Y'all know I'd like to stop an' tell ye a biggun', but I jest ain't got time right now."

"Well, why not?"

"Well, boys, y'all remember Aunt Sally?"

"Sure," came one response.

"I'm sorry to say she's passed away, and I waz a goin' to help the boys in her family dig her grave," said Uncle Bob as he continued to walk down the road. In those days it was customary for rural residents to work together when families needed help in preparing the grave of a loved one who had died.

"Hold on a minute an' we'll go help ye," one man said.

"Yeah. Hang on and let us get some hoes and shovels," said another.

The men ran to the local tool shed behind the house and returned with grave-digging tools. They hurried to catch Uncle Bob, still walking with the same unwavering pace.

After walking a about a mile or so, the men finally reached Aunt Sally's house, a small white building located not far from Uncle Bob's own home. There on the porch, as pretty as you please, sat Aunt Sally, healthy as a horse and grinnin' like a mule eating briars.

"Wait a minute!" shouted a surprised beholder. "I thought you said Aunt Sally had passed away."

"Well, boys," said Uncle Bob, with all the collected ease for which he was known. "You asked me to stop and tell y'all one o' my biggest and best lies and I just didn't have time to stop; so I told you the quickest lie I could come up with. And since y'all are here with hoes and shovels, we can go on up to the house and hoe my garden." And so they did. Sometimes lying can be a "very present help in trouble."[5]

---

[5] Psalms 46:1.

Uncle Pretty and the Commotion

Joyce Milligan Tatum

His real name was Wilbur, but we all called him "Pretty," and he was a Methodist minister in Florida. Uncle Pretty was a soft-spoken man, very sweet and gentle. He was married to my Mother's younger sister. He got the nickname "Pretty" when he was a young boy growing up in West Tennessee. He fell, one time, in a mud hole of considerable size; and the more he tried to get out, the more he slipped back in. When he finally did get out, he said to his friends who were laughing and making fun of him, "Now ain't I pretty?" The name stuck.

In Mason Hall where I grew up, we had three churches located right together. There were the Methodist, Cumberland Presbyterian, and Baptist churches, right across from each other, almost in a triangle shape. Since Mason Hall was so small, we were on a circuit where a minister only came one Sunday each month and he rotated every Sunday. One Sunday the Methodists would have the minister, and all three congregations attended "preaching." The next Sunday would be the Cumberland Presbyterians' turn for "preaching," and the next would be the Baptists. Every summer there was a big revival in the high school gym, and the churches took turns inviting a minister for the entire week of services. Every third summer the Methodists invited my Uncle Pretty because he was cheap and they didn't have to pay for his housing since he stayed with us.

Revivals in Mason Hall were big "to-do's," if you know what I mean. They began on Monday and would end on Friday nights with a big dinner that the whole community looked forward to every year. All the ladies would bring food. The men started early in the morning with their charcoal grills cooking everything from barbeque pork to goat. There were hamburgers and hot dogs for the kids, and the ladies would fry chickens. Fresh vegetables from the gardens and every kind of dessert that you could imagine was laid out on long tables in the school yard. The meals sometimes lasted longer that the preaching did.

The revival was in August that year, and Uncle Pretty had been called up from Florida by the Methodists to preach the revival in Mason Hall. On Thursday morning of that week he was worried because he had not had a single convert all week long. He was becoming concerned that his sermons were just not up to par. Uncle Pretty had a system for every revival. On Monday and Tuesday he preached from the Old Testament. On Wednesday and Thursday he preached from the New Testament, and on Friday nights he always preached from Revelation. Now Friday nights were his best nights, because he could preach hell fire and damnation better than any preacher anywhere around.

On Friday morning Uncle Pretty and I were out in the garden picking butterbeans for the community dinner that night. He was going over his sermon telling me highlights and getting it straight in his head. He was worried that if no one came forward that evening the Methodists would never invite him back for a revival, and he wouldn't get to see us so often. Ministers evidently pride themselves on being able to deliver the masses to the Lord. I thought long and hard on what he told me, and I decided to help him out a little. I had a roll of caps that I had stashed away. You know, the ones that went in the old cap guns. Any kind of pressure on those caps would set them off with a loud pop. When we got ready to go to the dinner I brought those caps with me. I had a plan.

Dinner was a huge success. The ladies had outdone themselves. They were all showing off their best homemade vegetables and desserts, and the men had so much meat prepared that I knew a lot of shut-ins were going to be eating well for several days when they got the leftovers.

Before the service I managed to sneak up to the front of the gym where metal chairs were placed on the gym floor for the people to sit during preaching. I took some of those caps and put them underneath the legs of various chairs. In our community during revival time, you always knew pretty well where certain people would sit. People are pretty predictable so I knew where most of the men would be sitting. The Baptists sat in the back. Cumberland Presbyterians sat in the middle, and the Methodists sat up front. On a hot summer night, after a big meal, I knew a lot of the men would be nodding off during the sermon. Uncle Pretty had that effect on a lot of people. Sure enough, when everyone began to gather for the preaching a number of men sat in those chairs under which I had placed those caps.

Kids back then sat in the bleachers. We didn't want to be anywhere near our parents. I found a bench near the top of the gym. Some of my friends motioned for me to come down with them and sit on some of the lower bleachers but I shook my head and faked like I had a bad headache.

The singing started, then the collection plates were passed and nothing happened. I figured I had messed up somehow; and soon, when Uncle Pretty started preaching, I settled in for another sermon. It was Friday night and he was preaching from Revelations! People began to squirm around. Then it happened. Mr. Boyd wiggled in that metal chair just enough to set off one of those caps. You should have heard it! It scared everyone, including me. His wife, Miss Ruth, gave him a look that would kill. A few folks snickered a little, but Uncle Pretty kept on. That was one thing about Uncle Pretty; no matter what happened around him, if he was caught up in a sermon, he was on a roll. You couldn't break his concentration, or his speed of delivery. He was preaching for all he was worth, making sure everyone (especially the Methodists) got their money's worth. The congregation settled back in. Suddenly two more of those caps went off. When someone turned to see who was making the noise, another one went off.

Now I had forgotten one thing. Those things stink! They don't just smell, they stink! They give off a sulfuric odor, and in a hot humid gym on an August night it was terrible. The only fan in the whole gym was up front keeping Uncle Pretty nice and cool. Thank goodness he was near the end of the sermon. When he offered up the "invitation," you should have seen the people going forward. It looked like half of the congregation was going up front to be saved; and if truth be known, that's exactly what they were doing, moving toward that fan trying to be "saved" from the smell of those caps. Uncle Pretty was delighted. He smiled from ear to ear. Never, as he later told us, had he had such a response to a sermon. He was overjoyed!

Since I was near the top of the bleachers, I got to witness the whole thing. The kids down below me were laughing for all it was worth; but I tried to keep a straight face, knowing if my father found out what I had done, I would be in for some serious punishment. Daddy looked up at me. We looked each other straight in the eye. HE KNEW!! I don't know how he knew, but he did. I could see it in his eyes. I could see it in his manner. I could tell by the way he straightened up in his chair and crossed his arms. I was a goner for sure. When we got home that night, Uncle Pretty was caught up in what had happened. He knew the Lord had worked a miracle and that the church would definitely invite him back for more revivals.

My father put his hand on my shoulder and said to Uncle Pretty, "Wilbur, you did a fine job, and we'll be sorry to see you leave for home tomorrow. Joyce here will be real sorry to see you go. In fact, she has volunteered to get up early in the morning and wash your car for you before breakfast. After that she is going to wash mine, and then she'll hoe the entire garden and pull all of the weeds from her Mother's flower beds. Why she even has volunteered to mow the yard too!"

"My goodness," said Uncle Pretty. "You will certainly have a busy day ahead of you young lady."

He leaned over to me and whispered in my ear "I love you dear child, and even though the good Lord said, 'A Little Child Shall Lead Them,' next time let me lead."

He kissed the top of my head; and, when I looked up, he winked. He too knew exactly what I had done.

The Preacher and Booger Swamp

Joyce Milligan Tatum

We were at church the Sunday when the preacher told us about the headless body floating through the air. I was sitting between Mama and Daddy, and my Grandma was in the pew in front of us. My little brother was next to me. I saw the preacher when he came in the door. Looked to me like he had tied one on the night before. His face was all drawn, and his eyes were bloodshot. He kept looking around like he was afraid something was going to get him. My Uncle Billy looks like that sometimes. Mama says Uncle Billy has a problem. Grandma says, "He's just high-strung." Daddy says, "He's strung out."

Anyway, when the preacher got up to the pulpit that Sunday morning he began to shake and jerk around. He looked like one of Granny's chickens when she chops off their heads. He couldn't stop shaking.

Preacher said he had been out on his horse riding the night before. He had been visiting over near White Plains. Everybody in town knew that is where the "still" is located. He said it was dark when he started for home and just as he got near the swamp over there, this headless body came floating toward him. It hung in the air for a while and came right up to him. The spirit tried to speak to him, but his horse got spooked and took off running. He had to hold on for dear life, so he said.

Everybody at church kind of avoided the preacher after that Sunday, and it wasn't long before the church leaders got together and held a church trial and expelled that preacher from the ministry. Other people have talked about seeing the spirit over there in Booger Swamp, but I ain't never seen it. And I hope I never do!

Lizzie and Jacob

Joyce Milligan Tatum

Her name was Lizzie. Elizabeth really, but Jacob called her Lizzie. They met in 1950. Jacob came to church one Sunday with Michael. Jacob was new to Cookeville, moving there from Harriman with his parents. His father had gotten a job at the hardware store located on the square. He and Michael lived on the same road and had become friends.

Jacob was very handsome with dark hair and the bluest eyes Lizzie had ever seen. She saw the boys when they first entered the church and wondered who the new boy was. They sat down on the pew next to Lizzie and her parents. She kept looking over at Jacob and once, he even caught her looking and winked. She was embarrassed and smitten at the same time.

After church was over he came up and introduced himself to her parents. Lizzie acted shy and wouldn't look up at him. That very afternoon, he came to her house and asked her father if he could take Lizzie on a date. Her father gave his permission and they began to "court." Lizzie said she fell in love with Jacob after the first week.

They dated for over a year before one Wednesday night after church, Jacob asked Lizzie out for Saturday night. He said he had something important to ask her. They made plans to have dinner at the B and B Restaurant. Jacob said to meet him there at seven. Lizzie was excited. The B and B Restaurant was one of the best eating establishments in town, and fancy too.

Lizzie didn't know that Jacob had already talked to her parents and had gotten their permission to ask her to marry him. He had even bought an engagement ring that he planned to give her that night. She got to the restaurant a little early and sat at a table at the front window in the corner so that she could watch for Jacob. Seven o'clock came and no Jacob – seven thirty, eight o'clock and then eight thirty. She was sitting there when her father came in a little before nine. She could tell he had been crying. His eyes were red and his shoulders were hunched over.

"He's gone, little girl," was all he could say.

Her Jacob had been killed in a car accident on his way to meet her. In his pocket was the engagement ring in a small white box tied with a blue ribbon.

Today the restaurant is long gone, but there are people who say that late at night when you round the corner from Jefferson Avenue onto Spring Street you can see Lizzie sitting at the corner table still waiting for her Jacob.

Dog-spell

Suellen Alfred and Danielle Aspinwall- Garman

(This story first appeared in *Teaching Through Stories: Yours, Mine, and Theirs*. Norwood, Massachusetts: Christopher-Gordon, 1998. It is used with permission.)

Annika, Danielle's daughter, was seven years old, precocious and persistent, energetic, amusing, and inventive. On a sunny Saturday in February, we went for a walk with Annika. "Tell me some words you want me to spell," Annika said. Annika was insatiable. Conversation was halted and incoherent, peppered with isolated words pronounced precisely by the adults, and with their spellings intoned by Annika. She showed no signs of fatigue with such a clever game.

Soon we were running out of words, but Annika was not running out of steam. She remained insistent. "Tell me another word," she said

"Annika, that's enough, now," said Danielle, her mother.

Annika ignored her mother's directive. "Give me another word." It was the chorus that answered all other elements of conversation.

At one point we rounded a bend and found a barking dog. With the hope that she could break the cycle of Annika's intractable spelling obsession, Suellen said, "Okay, now Annika, listen to that dog barking. Spell what that dog says." At that point, of course, the dog stopped barking. Annika leaned toward the animal with a determined look on her face.

"Bark again!" she demanded. The dog complied and barked again. Annika listened intently.

"A-R-F!" said Annika, inventively, and looked up in triumph at her mother and her friend. A smile of accomplishment spread across her upturned, shining face. And on we walked, spelling our way back home.

You Can't Even Spell

Blanche Nunnelley as told to Suellen Alfred

Your uncle Matt and I decided to bring some friends from Ohio down to East Tennessee where Matt said the fishing was especially good. A year or so ago he had gone fishing near a remote dock that was in the middle of nowhere Well, when we got onto some of those back roads outside of Knoxville, we got lost. We drove for a long time before saw even the first sign of a house. Of course Matt refused to stop to ask for direction. He used the excuse that he didn't want to march up the door of a total stranger just to ask how to get somewhere; so we just kept going, hoping that since there was a house nearby, there would soon be a store. Sure enough, not long after that we saw a small country store, with a rusting gasoline pump out front and an ancient dog sleeping by the door. By this time even Matt realized we needed some help.

We got out of the van to go ask for directions. The young woman behind the counter was very nice. I got the feeling she had seen lost "outlanders" like us before. When we asked her how to get to the dock Matt had fished from in the past, she said, "Go out of the parking lot and turn right," pronouncing the word "right" with that flat "i" that you hear all over East Tennessee. One of our friends from Ohio started laughing at her accent. "Raht? How do you spell that, "R - I - T - E?" he asked. It bothered me that he was mocking this young girl, but I wasn't bothered for long.

That self-assured young woman looked at him square in the eye like she wanted to slap his face. But she did something even better. With only the slightest smile she spoke in a thick Appalachian accent. "No wonder you're lawst," she said. "You cain't even spell."

Holy Christmas

Chester Goad

During my high school years, my family lived in an old historic home full of secret cracks and crevices, many of which were great for hiding. For me, the attic was the most alluring place in the house.

I was a good student, very active in clubs and organizations and marching band. I was also president of the Oneida High School student council. My parents thought I was just a great kid and never suspected me of any sneaky unbecoming behavior. They were wrong. Oh, I never did stupid things like smoke pot or drive too fast or get in fights, but I did have my secrets. My most ingenious secret would come blatantly back to haunt me in the most unexpected way. In fact, one could say it almost fell in my parents' lap. Who knew it would be something talked about and laughed about probably long after I am gone.

Even though I was involved in a number of extra-curricular activities, when I became a junior I began to hate school. There was just something about it that dampened my desire to go. So many times I just stayed home. May parents both worked outside the home, and because we lived not even 200 yards from my school, they trusted me to walk to school right down the street from the house. However, on more than one occasion I had other plans. One particularly fateful morning, I got up early with them and got dressed as I always did. They usually left around 8:00 a.m. As they drove out of sight, I waved a sincere good-bye. Then, I would strip out of my school clothes into something more "home worthy" and relax.

My only problem was the time they came home for lunch breaks. But I had a plan for that situation. Behind the bathroom closet was a secret ladder that either my parents had not found or would never think to check. At lunch time, I would take a few books or magazines, climb that secret ladder into the attic, and read leisurely until I heard both cars load up and drive out of sight. Free at last, I would go back down the ladder to the TV or stereo and my afternoon activities. Occasionally, if the phone rang, I would screen the calls. If I saw that the school was calling to check on me, I would immediately take on my devastatingly sick voice and proceed to explain the illness that kept me home that day. I became very good at sounding pitiful. I was never found out – that is until Christmas break of my freshman year in college.

My parents were in the middle of selling our home after some financial trouble. It was probably our saddest Christmas ever. Soon we would move from that rambling old house into another place. As I thought about the move, I began to wonder if I had ever left books or magazines up there. The idea began to rattle me. I just had to find out. In a few days we would be moved.

I decided I would go "take a shower." Actually, I decided to turn the shower on and let it run while I climbed up the old ladder behind the linen closet and looked for any forgotten items. I turned the shower on full blast, opened the linen closet, and climbed to the attic. I began to search. So far so good. What was that? I thought I saw something over in a darkened unfloored part of the attic. I tried to be very quiet. I took a giant step onto a two-by-four in between rows of insulation.

I was sure I was going to be able to pull this off. But somehow I lost my balance and fell. The floor beneath me crumbled. I began to fall right through the ceiling of the room below. I could feel my legs dangling beneath me. Down stairs, my father was sitting in his recliner when the ceiling gave way with two legs dangling from the ceiling over his head. I tried to grab the two-by-four. Stupidly I thought if I could at least get a hold of the beam and pull myself up, maybe they wouldn't know it was me. Sadly, I seriously overestimated my strength. I simply could not pull myself back up into the attic. I would pull myself up and fall, pull, fall, pull, and fall. It seemed like an eternity until I heard a booming voice bellow, "Just let go!!" I was defeated. I let go and fell what seemed to be a thousand feet and landed directly in front of my father.

"Holy Christmas!" he yelled, glaring at me as pieces of insulation and dust continued to tumble down on my body covered with white powder.

My mother came running from the other room. "Are you all right?" she asked. I nodded. "Then just don't even talk to me!" She said as she walked out of the room furiously trying to hold her tongue until later.

My father then said sternly that he did not even want to know why I was up there until the mess was cleaned up. Some folks would be coming to appraise the house in just minutes.

I have never cleaned, duct taped, and painted so fast in all my life. I did so as my brothers looked on and laughed with snide little cat grins. I had been caught. The day of reckoning for perfect child Chester had arrived. I had fallen from grace.

I remember later explaining the whole story about skipping school and hiding from them in the attic. It hurt to see the disappointment in their faces. We later laughed about the whole event. We still laugh. I will never forget my daddy's booming voice as he bellowed, "Holy Christmas!" My falling through the ceiling had indeed made it a "holey" Christmas. But the best thing was, in spite of all that happened, after the shock wore off, the disaster was a kind of comic relief that alleviated some of the stress that families go through when it is time to move.

The Christmas Tree

Joyce Milligan Tatum

I remember the day he left for the Air Force. We drove him over to the bus station, Momma, Daddy, and me.

"Be good, kid" he said as he hugged me hard and tight.

I kissed him on the cheek and said, "I love you."

My Dad shook his hand and my Mother, usually a reserved sort of lady cried quiet tears. "Be safe," she said as she hugged and kissed him.

As he boarded the Greyhound bus bound for Memphis he turned and waved good-bye. It was May of 1965. The start of summer in West Tennessee. Ronnie had just graduated from high school and decided that the Air Force was the place he wanted to be. He could get a degree, see the world, and be part of a great adventure. Little did we know that a little Southeast Asian country would become so important in our lives.

Regular letters came from Ronnie. Letters about basic training, his friends, and things he did and saw. He ended up at an Air Force base in Fort Worth, Texas. To a nine-year girl, it seemed like a world away. I wrote to him, told him about the start of school, my friends, what the weather was like. Days turned into weeks and weeks into a year. Soon it was summer again. Letters still arrived regularly from Ronnie.

One letter in particular worried my Mother. I remember the day it arrived. I had been picking butter beans when the mail came. The garden ran along side of the road so I saw the mailman in his green car coming. I ran to meet him knowing he always had a stick of gum for me.

"Looks like you got another letter from your brother," he said.

"Thanks, Mr. Frank," I said to him as I took the mail and the gum he offered.

"Tell your Mama 'Hello' for me," he replied.

"I sure will," I told him. I ran into the house with the mail.

"Mama, Mama," I called out "Mail's here. Letter from Ronnie." I threw the mail down on the couch in the living room and headed out to the kitchen to get a drink. Mama came into the kitchen behind me with the mail and sat down at the table. She opened the letter and began to read.

"Joyce, go get your old geography book, the one with the map of the world in it."

"I don't know where it is," I said looking in the refrigerator for a piece of cheese.

Using a tone of voice I had never heard before, she said, "Go get it now." Pulling my head out of the refrigerator, I gave her a puzzled look and went after the book. When I found it I brought it back into the kitchen.

"Why do you want this ole thing?" I asked.

She took it from me and immediately opened it to a world map. She ran her finger over the page looking for something. Muttering under her breath and ignoring me she said, "It must be here somewhere. There it is."

"What are you looking for and why?" I wanted to know.

"Your brother is being sent to the Philippines for three months and then on to someplace called Cambodia."

"Wow, can we go visit him there? Where is it? Show me."

She was studying the map hard. I looked down over her shoulder to the spot where she had her finger.

"What's that country next to it?" I asked.

Suddenly her face changed again to one of fear.

"It's Vietnam. The place we see on the news every night. That's where all that fighting is. Where all those people are getting killed. Now, go outside and play," she replied. "Go on," she said "Out! Pick the rest of the beans, go play, do something." I could tell she was thinking about Ronnie. When my father came home from work they went into their bedroom with Ronnie's letter. Later my father came out and began to fix dinner.

"What's going on?" I asked him. "Where's Mama? Is she sick?"

To see my father in the kitchen during the workweek usually meant my Mom was sick. Saturday was his day to make dinner.

"Help me here, kiddo," he said. "Your Mom is resting. She's had a hard day."

"No, she didn't. She's not done anything today since the mail came. She's worried about Ronnie, isn't she?"

"How much do you know?" he asked.

"I know he's going to some place called Cambodia and that it's close to Vietnam. Why does that matter? He's not going to be doing something dangerous, is he?"

"Maybe," my father replied. He began to make grilled cheese sandwiches and grabbed a can of soup from the cabinet. "Your brother is a lineman in communications. It's his job to make sure the lines are up and stay up so that other soldiers can communicate with each other."

"So?" I replied as I watched him.

"So, it can be dangerous work. You can't carry a gun and work on a line at the same time when you are up a pole 15 feet in the air. There are people called snipers who don't want you putting up the lines. It's dangerous work."

"You mean someone might try to hurt him?" I asked.

He nodded. "Let's eat now and worry later O.K?"

"O.K., Daddy"

Days turned into weeks and the letters became infrequent. Mama began to watch for the mailman every day and sometimes would even meet him at the mailbox. Many days he simply shook his head and reached from the car window to touch my Mama's arm in sympathy. On days when a letter did arrive, he would begin to blow his car horn when he turned on our street. When she heard the horn, Mama was waiting at the mailbox happy and excited.

Ronnie spent six weeks in the Philippines and in a letter told us that he had been sent on to Cambodia. Each night the news seemed filled with the number of causalities and the strange sounding names of far off cities and towns. If anything was said of Cambodia my parents would lean in to listen closer. They were listening for the names of towns Ronnie spoke of in his letters home. I started back to school worried about Ronnie but not as concerned as my Mother. I knew that Ronnie, ten years older than me, was invincible. My big brother came to my rescue when things went wrong; he knew how to build me a playhouse from old wood that Daddy had; he would carry me outside after a storm to splash in the rain and mud puddles; he taught me to ride a bike, and would let me ride home with him from school in his beloved car, stopping by the store to get me a Coke and Crackerjacks. Nothing could happen to him. He was perfect.

One early fall afternoon just as I was getting off the school bus a black car pulled up beside me.

"Hi there little lady," a man called out.

I turned around to see two men in Air Force uniforms sitting there.

The one who called out to me asked, "Are you a Milligan? Do you live around here?"

"Yes sir. We live right there," I said, pointing to the house.

"Is your Mama home?" he wanted to know.

"Yep, why?"

"We need to see her," he replied. He pulled his head back into the car and they drove into the driveway. As they were getting out of the car, I began to run up on the porch. My mother stepped out of the front door to face them.

"Mama?" I asked seeing her face. "What's wrong?"

I looked from her to them. One man had a briefcase which he opened pulling an official looking letter out. "Ma'am," he began "Your son is in a hospital back in the Philippines. He is seriously ill. We are here to bring this letter to you stating his condition."

"He's not dead?" she asked looking confused.

"No, but he is very ill. We expect he will make a full recovery, but it will take a while."

"He's not dead?" she asked again.

"No ma'am. Here are the phone numbers of the Red Cross so that you can get in touch with them and with him."

"He's not dead," she said again looking from them to me and back again. She took the letter from the officer and thanked him. Her whole look had changed from fear to jubilation.

"Mama," I said again. "Did you hear that? He's not dead, just real sick.

"Oh! Praise the Lord." She began to cry.

The men soon left. She opened the letter and read it and immediately called the Red Cross. The woman she spoke to took down the information and promised to call her back the next day. When my father got home she told him what had happened.

 After she went into the kitchen I asked my father, "Why is Mama so happy? Ronnie is really sick and in the hospital. I don't understand. Looks to me like she should be sad."

My father smiled and hugged me tight. "Someday you'll understand."

Ronnie spent two weeks in the hospital suffering from a severe intestinal blockage that required major surgery and another four weeks recovering. He was getting a leave to come home for Christmas. Never mind that he would have to go back to Cambodia, he was coming home. My parents were very excited.

That was the year of the silver Christmas tree. My father found it in a store in Union City. An ugly thing, I thought, but Daddy said it was the newest and latest thing. A small wheel with various colors turned on an axle in front of a light which projected various colors onto the tree. A silver tree that changed from yellow to red to green to blue. A silver tree with branches sticking out straight. A silver tree! How un-Christmas could you get!!

The big day arrived. My mother had been baking for three days. Everything Ronnie had ever expressed a liking to had either been made or the ingredients were in the kitchen waiting to be made. German chocolate cake, coconut cake, pecan pie, apple pie, banana split cake, sugar cookies, tea cakes, brownies, tea with sugar in it - all awaiting his arrival. Daddy picked him up at the station. When he got home, he looked different. His hair was cut short, he was thinner.

Still his hugs were the same. And he was carrying a bunch of Christmas presents.

"Hey there," he called out when he saw me. He bent down on one knee to hug me.

"Seems like ages, since I last saw you. I brought you something," he said.

"I don't need nothin'," I said, excited at the thought. I laughed because I knew his "something for me" was already under the tree. Daddy had brought packages in first and then gone back out to help Ronnie bring in his duffel bags.

"O. K," he answered as he rumpled my hair.

He turned to see my mother standing at the door of the kitchen. With her hand to her heart she sobbed his name. He quietly went over to her and literally picked her off the floor in a hug and kiss.

"Hi Mama. It sure is good to be home." She stroked his short hair and touched his cheek.

"I've missed you," she said. "Are you hungry? I've made some dinner. Some of your favorites. You look thin. You cut your hair." Short little sentences all strung together came out of her mouth at once.

"It sure is good to be home," he said again, this time with a laugh.

As my mother put the finishing touches on dinner, Ronnie took one of his duffel bags to his room. I followed him with the other one. He asked about school, my friends, easy-going questions and answers. He went into the living room and saw the tree.

"Wow! Whose idea was that?" he asked.

Trying to make the best of it I said, "What do you think? Cool huh? Daddy got it."

Ronnie looked at it again and then at me. I plugged in the color wheel.

Putting on a brave front I said, "It's really great, don't you think?"

"That is about the ugliest tree I have ever seen," he said. "Where's the real tree? What's Christmas without a green tree? I've been half way around the world, and I've never seen any trees that look like that."

I was already feeling pretty bad about the tree and now I felt worse. "Daddy got it," was all I could say.

"Ah, it's all right, I guess," he said. "Sure is different though. Doesn't make it feel like Christmas though, does it?" I saw the look on his face.

Daddy came into the room. "What do you think?" Daddy asked. "Latest thing. No mess to clean up. No sap. Easy to store and can be used year after year." He sounded like the salesman from the store repeating the words.

"Wow, Daddy," was all Ronnie could say.

Mama called out, "Supper's ready. C'mon and eat while it's hot."

Ronnie was the first to the table. We bowed our heads for the prayer that Daddy said. I glanced sideways at Ronnie who was looking at each of us with amazement, and I could tell he really was glad to be home.

It turned cold that night. Very cold! "Burr," I shivered the next morning. "Don't we have any heat?" I asked.

"Hush up. You'll wake up your brother. Of course we have heat. It just takes a little time to warm up this old house," Mama said. "Go put on some socks." I went back into my bedroom, grabbed some thick socks from the drawer and a stocking cap. I crammed the hat on my head and put the socks on.

"Now I'm warmer," I announced going back into the dining room.

"Silly," my Mama said as she playfully hit me on the head with a potholder. Ronnie came into the room and began to laugh.

"I like your outfit. Dig it out of the rag bag?"

"I'm cold," I replied. "I bet it snows."

Ronnie looked out the window longingly. "Sure hope it does. Where I've been, they've read about snow but have never seen it."

"You're kidding, right?" I couldn't believe anyone had never seen snow, except if you lived someplace like Florida or South America. He pulled the cap over my eyes.

"Some people don't have near as much as you do, 'little bit,' and they sure don't know anything about our weather. They don't understand a tornado or snow. They live on fish and rice. They have never tasted chocolate or tea or apples. They live in one-room shacks, and have no pillows and blankets. They don't have toys like you do. Little girls don't have dolls over there. They don't have Christmas trees or Santa Claus. Most of them don't even have shoes."

I couldn't imagine such a place. Mama brought in our breakfast plates. She had fixed bacon and eggs along with biscuits and gravy. "There is more food on this plate than some of those people see all day," he said. "Thank you, Mama."

"What are you going to do today?" she asked him.

"I thought I'd go see some of my old friends. Hang out for a while. Do you need me to do something?" he asked her.

"No," she answered. "Don't stay out to long. You need your rest. Remember you just got out of the hospital."

He smiled at her "I'm fine. I'll be back early. Before dark, I promise. I'm not going to miss one of your suppers."

She smiled and patted his hand. After breakfast I cleaned off the table and took the dishes into the kitchen to be washed. I went off to my room and made the bed. I heard Ronnie talking to Mama, and soon the front door closed. My room looked out over the driveway, and I saw him get into his old car. He sat there for a minute and then started it up and left. I got dressed and went into the living room where the Christmas tree stood.

"Stupid old tree," I muttered to it. "You are soooo ugly!" I thought about the kids in the countries where Ronnie had been. I would sure be willing to give them this old tree I thought. Silver!!

As the day wore on it seemed to get colder. Snow was on the way for sure I thought. That afternoon since school was out for the holiday, I went for a walk on Mr. Ray's farm. Mr. Ray had over 100 acres of farmland that bordered our property. Most of it was cleared for planting. Soybeans and corn mostly. In the winter the land lay barren. Up and down the fence rows, rabbits would scurry out and about. Sometimes I could chase a rabbit all over a field. Never caught one, but there was always that outside chance that someday I would. I had gone about a half mile up one fence row when I saw it - a perfect green Christmas tree. I had been up and down that fence row for years and had never noticed that tree. Where did it come from? How long had it been there? I couldn't believe it. There it stood all alone as though it were waiting for me. I looked around as if I might get caught. The perfect tree – right there – on the fence row. I turned around and headed for home looking back over my shoulder every few feet to make sure it was still there. Ronnie was already home when I got there.

"Look at you," Mama said.

"Where have you been?" Ronnie asked. "Your nose looks like Rudolph's and your hands are freezing! Didn't you wear any gloves?"

"My goodness," Mama answered. "Go wash your hands and face in warm water and make sure you dry off good. You are going to get sick right here before Christmas." I did as I was told. As I stood there letting the warm water run over my hands I tried to think of a way to get my tree home and the silver tinsel one out of the house. Daddy came home and said it was snowing just a few miles from the house. Just as we sat down for dinner big white flakes began their slow decent to the ground.

"Look!" I called out. "Look it's snowing!" I ran to the window. Now it was beginning to feel like Christmas. That night, all snug in my bed, I thought about the tree and tried to think of a way to get it home. I wanted it to be a surprise on Christmas morning. When the morning came around, the ground was white with snow. I jumped out of bed and went running to the window. Then I went running to Ronnie's room.

"Look! Look!" I shouted. "It snowed." Ronnie moaned and rolled over on his stomach. "Get up, c'mon! Snow!" I ran to his window to look out.

Just as I turned around a pillow caught me upside the head. "Ouch!" I yelled. "Hey!"

I picked up the pillow and threw it back at him. Soon, one of our old fashioned pillow fights began in earnest. Amidst the giggles and muffled shrieks, Mama walked in.

"You two stop it before you bust one of my pillows," she shouted.

"Oops, sorry," I said as I accidentally hit her with a misplaced pillow. Soon she had joined in the fight. Ronnie managed to capture all of the pillows and won the battle. Mama threatened to tell Santa on Ronnie and me if we didn't stop misbehaving.

"Get up," she said breathing heavily "Your breakfast is getting colder by the minute. In the kitchen with both of you in ten minutes.

I mean it. I have a lot to do today." She picked up a pillow and with a good aim hit Ronnie. He laughed out loud.

"After breakfast will you go out with me to play in the snow?" I asked him.

"Only if you bundle up good," he said.

"Beat you to the kitchen," I said as I raced for the door.

"I have to get up first," was all I heard.

Soon after breakfast I bundled up in a coat, scarf, hat and gloves. Ronnie dug in his closet and found some of his old winter clothes and did the same. We pulled out the wooden sled from the garage, and with me riding along he began to pull the sled out into the farm. We built a snowman, a snow fort. He watched me make snow angels and threw snowballs when he thought I wasn't looking. It felt good to have my brother back. Close to lunchtime Ronnie complained about being cold so we started for home. This time I helped him pull the sled. Walking along the fence row, he spotted the tree.

"Would you look at that," he said. "I never noticed that tree there before. I've been hunting all up and down this fence row for years and never even noticed that tree."

The evergreen tree stood about seven feet tall and had a perfect shape to it. The lowest branches were a least a foot off the ground and each one looked as if it has been placed on the tree with careful precision. Right at the top a single branch stood up, just perfect for a star, I thought.

"Sure is pretty," I said. "Much better than that ole' silver one we have".

Ronnie chuckled and nodded. "C'mon," he said, "I'm getting cold. Let's get home."

We trudged back to the house and got our wet things off. Mama had lunch ready.

After lunch Ronnie went to his room to read. I followed him in and lay down across his twin bed letting my feet and hands dangle over the sides.

"I wish we had our old green Christmas tree back. Why did Daddy have to get that silver one? I don't like it." I stated.

"It's O.K.," he said. "Not really like Christmas though, without a green tree. Guess I'll miss it too. That will be some memory for me to take back." He chuckled and went back to his reading.

I watched him quietly. "I'll miss you when you go back. Don't get hurt over there, O.K?"

He looked up again and then got up from his chair and sat down beside me on the bed. I climbed into his lap and snuggled up to him.

"It's all right. I have to do what I do. It's my job. I can't promise I won't get hurt or even worse; but you have to know, 'little bit,' that I love you and Mama and Daddy. If something happens to me you have to remember that. Promise?"

I hugged him tight. "I promise," I whispered. He rocked me back and forth; and sometime later, he laid me down on his bed and covered me with a quilt. I napped while he read. When I woke up he was gone. I went into the kitchen.

"Well hello, sleepyhead," Mama said. "Have a nice nap?"

"I guess," I answered. "Where's Ronnie?"

"He said he had something to do. I saw him in Daddy's tool shed about a half hour ago." I grabbed my coat and went running out the door. When I got to the shed the light was on, but Ronnie was nowhere to be seen. I searched around the house, but he wasn't there. I stumbled back inside.

"He's gone somewhere," I said.

Mama looked up from her baking. "Well, he'll be back. Your Daddy will be home early today. It is Christmas Eve. We'll have dinner early before the caroling."

It had become our tradition to go Christmas caroling along our street each year. Neighbors would join in so that by the time we reached the last homes there would be some 10 to 15 people. The last stop was always "Miss" Mary's house where she invited everyone in for hot chocolate and cookies. She was a widow with grown children who couldn't come home for Christmas, so our stop at her house was always a treat for her and us.

"Here," Mama said, "help me with this frosting. I'm making a cake to take over to Miss Mary's house. I think a lot of our neighbors will want to see your brother tonight, and I don't want Miss Mary to run out of food." We worked for a while chit-chatting about Christmas and what Santa might bring. Mama knew I didn't really believe in Santa, but she pretended. She always said Santa was a spirit that moved real people to do good things for others. She described him as a kind of Christmas angel that just happened to be dressed in red. A little while later, Ronnie came in huffing and puffing from the cold.

"Where have you been?" I asked him.

"Out for a walk sleepyhead," he answered as he rubbed his cold hands across my cheeks.

"Ugh!! You're all cold! Mama!" I shrieked.

"Here, stop it you two." She laughed out loud. "I swear. You are always at each other. Ronnie, stop bothering your sister and go warm up." She smiled at him as he kissed her cheek.

"Got it," he said. She nodded.

"Got what?" I asked.

"Nothing" they answered together.

"Set the table," Mama said. "Your Daddy will be home any minute." Just then he walked in the door.

"Told you," she said with a wink.

I hurried to set the table and forgot all about their conversation. Soon afterwards we sat down to eat an early supper.

"Daddy, Ronnie and I saw the perfect Christmas tree this morning," I said.

"You did. Let me guess. It's right there in the living room," he replied.

"No. It's out on Mr. Ray's fence row."

"Well, we'll have to look at it for next year won't we? We have a perfectly good one right now," he answered. I knew not to say anything else.

After supper dishes were washed, Mama sent me to bundle up for caroling. While I was putting on my boots I started thinking about the tree. I wanted to do something special for Ronnie. Something he would remember all year. Why couldn't I get that tree and put it up as a surprise for him? Daddy wouldn't have to do any of the work. I could do it all by myself, or so I thought. I knew everyone would get caught up in the caroling and wouldn't even notice if I disappeared for a while. I thought I could get everything done in a short amount of time and could get back to Miss Mary's house before anyone really missed me. I finished getting on my coat, scarf and gloves and announced that I was going to go outside.

"You'll get cold," my Mama warned.

I went out the front door and in the early twilight could see the outline of the shed. Looking over my shoulder to make sure no one saw me I made a beeline for the shed. Inside I found my Daddy's hatchet. I brought it outside and hid it under a bush close to the corner of the house. Soon Mama, Daddy and Ronnie came out, and we went next door. The Hurleys came outside as soon as we began the second verse of "O, Come All Ye Faithful." As soon as we ended, we exchanged Christmas greetings and all went on to the Wagner's house.

Mr. Hester came out and in his big booming voice shouted "Merry Christmas." After a chorus of "Away in the Manger," he grabbed his coat and shut the door.

"Where's Dottie?" my Mama asked?

"She's going to meet us over at Miss Mary's house," he answered. "She is making a batch of brownies and said she'd see us there."

Now was my chance to slip away. While Mr. Hester and Ronnie and my Daddy were talking and walking, I hung back and slowed down. At the Farris house I was well out of light range but close enough that my Mama could see me when she looked back. As soon as she turned back around to begin singing, I took off back to the house. I grabbed the hatchet from under the bush and got the sled from the porch where Ronnie and I had left it. I started off toward the fence row.

The night was clear and cold. The snow that was left had turned into a slippery icy sheet especially in the field. It reflected the light of the moon so brightly I could see my way fairly clear. I pulled the sled after me and started hunting for the tree. I kept thinking I would come upon it any minute. It had to be here somewhere. The stars were so bright and the air so cold that I could see my breath. Ice crystals began to form on my cheeks from the tears I started shedding. I couldn't find the tree anywhere.

"It has to be here. It has to!" I muttered. "It's my special present for Ronnie. Where is it?" All up and down that fence row I searched.

Not once but twice. Had someone else gotten the tree? I finally discovered the spot where the tree had stood. It had been cut down cleanly. Only a stump was left. I sat down and cried great racking tears of grief. The one gift I could have given my big brother. The gift of the tree was gone.

"What on earth are you doing out here, little bit?" my brother said softly.

He had come upon me quietly and sat down on the sled. I climbed up in his lap and began to cry even more. Between my sobs I told him how I had wanted the tree for him. How I had wanted to make it a special Christmas. He hugged me tight and kissed the top of my head.

"Don't you know what is special? Just being home makes it a special Christmas. I never thought I would miss this place so much and you and Mama and Daddy. I've been memorizing everything you guys say and do so that I can remember it all when I lie awake at night missing you. Don't worry about the tree. You are what makes my Christmas special. Let's go before Mama misses both of us and we get into trouble. C'mon." He sat me on the ground and knelt down.

"Get on. I'll give you a piggy-back ride." I climbed on his back and he reached down for the hatchet. "You were going to cut down that tree with Daddy's hatchet," he asked?

Still sniffling I nodded. He shook his head.

"Good thing I found you when I did. You might have ended up chopping off a finger or a toe. We'd better put this back before Daddy gets after you for messing in his tool shed." When we got back to the house he put the hatchet away and left the sled near the porch. Up the street we went to Miss Mary's house. He sat me down on her porch.

"I bet Mama has some cocoa for you inside. I'll be back. Get me a cup too, little bit," he said. I kissed him on the cheek and turned to go inside the house. As I was opening the screen door I turned to see him watching me.

"Go on," he waved. He threw me a kiss. I went inside.

"There you are," Mama said. "Here is a cup of chocolate for you." She bent down and kissed the top of my head. Daddy and Mr. Hester were discussing the war and what an impact it was having on the economy. Neighbors were smiling and wishing each other a Merry Christmas. Ronnie came in and whispered something to Mama. A soft look came over her face and she hugged him and smiled at me. Soon he was caught up in conversations with neighbors who were wishing him well and asking questions about his military assignments. Children began to yawn, and soon people began to drift home. Mama helped Miss Mary clean up, and on our way out she slipped a package under her tree for her. I noticed other small gifts from friends and neighbors. With a frown I realized I had forgotten to check under our tree to see if there was a present for me. I said something to that effect to Mama on the way home. She announced that under no circumstances would anybody be allowed to see the tree that night. "You are going straight to bed," she announced.

"But Mama," I protested.

"No," she answered. "Straight to bed." We came in the back door and she hustled me into the bathroom to change into my pajamas. When I came out she was still standing there.

"I'll tuck you in tonight," she said. She heard my prayers and read me the Christmas story from the Bible.

"Now good night," she whispered to me. "I love you."

"I love you, too," I murmured back. Soon I was fast asleep. The next morning I was awake by 6:00. The rule at our house was that no one was allowed up out of bed until Daddy got up.

"Daddy, are you awake yet?" I called loudly.

"No," my Father answered. I heard my brother laugh.

"Will you please get up," I called out?

"No," he answered again. My brother laughed again. Ten minutes passed (it seemed like 30).

"Now will you get up?" I called out. I heard Daddy's feet hit the floor. Ten more minutes passed and he came to the door.

"All right you can get up now." He yawned.

Mama had been up already and had coffee ready. I stood at the door of the living room that had been kept shut all night. Daddy stood at the door with his coffee cup in hand.

"I suppose you want to go in?" he asked. "Well I need another cup of coffee first." He started to walk to the kitchen.

"Daddy!!" I whined.

"Oh, all right," he said as he opened the door.

I stood there for a few minutes.

"What? How?" was all I could say.

There standing in the middle of the room was Ronnie's tree. Ronnie was next to it grinning from ear to ear.

"Beat you to it, little bit," he said.

The most beautiful tree in the whole world was standing right there. I had wanted it to be my present to Ronnie, but he had gotten it for me. I ran to him, and he knelt down to embrace me. I buried my face in his neck and cried.

"Merry Christmas, little sister," was all he could say.

I don't remember much more about that day. I can't even tell you what I got from Santa. But I can tell you what I got from my big brother. The most wonderful and beautiful gift in the world. Love.

www.ingramcontent.com/pod-product-compliance
Lightning Source LLC
Chambersburg PA
CBHW070014140726
47908CB00020B/1423